GRACE REGIFTED

A JOURNEY OF FORGIVENESS

Bethany Albright

WESTBOW
PRESS®
A DIVISION OF THOMAS NELSON
& ZONDERVAN

WestBow Press books may be ordered through booksellers or by contacting:

WestBow Press
A Division of Thomas Nelson & Zondervan
1663 Liberty Drive
Bloomington, IN 47403
www.westbowpress.com
844-714-3454

Scripture quotations are from the ESV® Bible (The Holy Bible, English Standard Version®), copyright © 2001 by Crossway, a publishing ministry of Good News Publishers. Used by permission. All rights reserved

The author used a pen name.

ISBN: 978-1-6642-2229-8 (sc)
ISBN: 978-1-6642-2231-1 (hc)
ISBN: 978-1-6642-2230-4 (e)

Library of Congress Control Number: 2021902038

Print information available on the last page.

WestBow Press rev. date: 02/24/2021

To my family

PROLOGUE

Brooke
August 2023
Dallas, Texas

From across the massive, marble-embellished courtroom, I scrutinize him. The stark lighting exacerbates his angular jaw, which he clenches while staring aimlessly into space. The wrinkles across his forehead and under his eyes add at least a decade to his twenty-nine years.

Awaiting the verdict, a rush of emotions threatens to overwhelm me. I want mercy for the accused, but I know the law and appreciate the legal system. It's in place to protect society. Plus, there's the issue of a revolving door of repeat offenders, like this guy.

The verdict will inevitably be guilty. The evidence we presented was insurmountable. But my question is, what will the sentence be? I hold a deep hope that it includes a prison ministry that draws this lost soul to Christ.

The accused turns his head slightly and shoots a side glare at me. His penetrating eyes seem to hold dark secrets. Shivers skitter along my skin.

"Brooke, are you all right?"

I shut my eyes hard, then open them wide to look at my brother-in-law, John, seated next to me. "Yeah, just lost in thought."

John places his hand momentarily over mine.

I force a smile to reassure him that I'm fine. He pulls out a legal pad and makes his pen fly across the paper.

John appears distinguished with his salt-and-pepper hair. He started graying in his thirties, and I've wondered lately whether the early graying was due to being married to my occasionally intense older sister, Abbey, or the demands of being an attorney. Maybe a combination.

John pushes the paper across the polished mahogany toward me. I read: *Don't worry—we'll negotiate a reduced sentence contingent on agreement to participate in Christian prison ministry.*

I nod.

We are senior partners in our family business, Conrad and Townsend Law Firm, and work together on cases that require our different skills and expertise. For this trial, John has more experience in criminal law than I do. But I contribute my personal experience, formed by events I lived through in college. For this case, my experience outweighs my law degree.

I glance back to my dad seated behind us. He founded our law firm and retired five years ago, turning over the reins to me, his thirty-five-year-old daughter, and John, his forty-year-old son-in-law. Dad is absolutely beaming, I'm sure with pride in John and me, because he sees this trial as a sure win.

I view it as rightful closure for the victim's family. Hopefully, this trial serves as a warning to potential perpetrators of drug-facilitated date rape, and a means of protection for women.

But it is also the trial of a human life suspended. It's suspended between a choice of repentance or repeated rebellion, not just against society, but against Christ. With Christ, it means eternal life; without Christ, it means eternal death.

Waiting for the jury to return to the courtroom, my thoughts wander. Memories of events from almost two decades ago flood my mind. The memories are so vivid, it's as if the events occurred yesterday.

PART

I

Brooke

1

Mom sat in my retro metal desk chair, clasping her hands. I was certain her rigid posture wasn't just because the chair was uncomfortable. Her sunken cheeks and hollowed eyes resembled those of a loved one sitting on the front pew at a funeral.

"So, Brooke, this calendar of events says there's a mandatory resident's meeting at ten tomorrow morning and—" Kara stopped mid-sentence, studying my face, which must have shown worry. She diverted her attention to the subject of my gaze: Mom.

I knew Mom was dreading her impending departure. Over the past several months, Mom and I had been together almost nonstop, shopping for dorm accessories. Since shopping wasn't Kara's thing, Mom and I had fun, just the two of us, hunting for the perfect décor to make my dorm room look chic yet comfy. Well, except for my new retro chair, which was not comfy. I wouldn't be dozing off while studying at that desk.

Dad was probably more than ready to hit the road after assembling a cheap bookcase that required an unexpected trip to Home Depot on a hunt for a missing nut-and-bolt combo. He'd finally completed the tedious job without spouting even one of his typical expletives.

With his commanding attorney voice, he announced, "Margie, it's time for us to get on the road. We have over a three-hour drive ahead of us, and I have an early morning case."

Yep, pretty sure Mom already knew all of that, but she nodded docilely, mustering a weak smile. I'd come to realize over the years that Dad's bravado when making announcements was a way to get noticed and take control of a situation, especially when he felt uncomfortable. This time, his discomfort probably stemmed from a combined irritation of having to deal with the bookcase while listening to our incessant girl talk.

I jumped up out of a sense of duty. "Aw, thank you, Mom and Dad, for everything."

Tears welled in Mom's eyes as Dad crossed the room and pulled me into a hug. He cleared his throat. "You call us if you need anything, sweetheart."

Mom hugged me too, and the familiar scent of her Chanel perfume was comforting. She could only manage a whispered, "Love you." I couldn't deny the lump in my throat as they turned to leave.

But wow! I thought they'd never leave! I appreciated all that they'd done to make the dorm room look amazing, but I was more than ready to get started with college life.

I watched Kara unpack her clothes. Even though her dad had paid for half of our room's stuff, he left as soon as he'd unloaded Kara's heavy moving boxes. Kara was tough, though. Since she'd lost her mom to cancer five years ago, she'd been pretty much on her own. Her dad obviously loved her; it was just that he was a dad, clueless about how to take on the role of a mom. After her mom died, Kara had put on at least twenty pounds, which was noticeable since she was only five foot two. But once she became involved in high school activities, which included joining the debate team with me, she slimmed down.

Kara and I kept a low-profile in high school, unlike my sister Abbey, who was in a million clubs and left behind a closet full of homecoming and prom dresses. We were asked out to school dances, but neither of us dated anyone special. When we weren't studying, most of our time was spent at debate tournaments.

"Kara! My parents are gone! We're officially University of Texas Longhorns! Let's go meet some guys!"

Kara snickered. "Hold on, party animal. I need to finish unpacking."

"I want a social life while I'm still young." Flying to the window and throwing back our new lacy sheers, I saw students bustling on the lawns below.

"I realize we need better social lives, Brooke. Let's just don't do anything crazy or sleazy."

"Of course not, but don't you think it'd be fun to date a bunch of different guys—hopefully, sweet and considerate ones? If they also turn out to be cute, that'd be amazing. Especially considering how plain-looking I am."

"Brooke! Stop putting yourself down. You do that all the time."

"Hey, you're an only child, so you have no idea what it's like to be the little sister of drop-dead gorgeous Abbey."

"Stop comparing yourself to her. Life will be better for you . . . and me." Kara winked and gave a crooked grin.

My shoulders dropped. "You're right. Thanks for always putting up with my quirks. You're more like a sister to me than Abbey." I heaved open the heavy window with a rush of adrenaline. My shoulders rose as I breathed in the warm afternoon air. I yelled to the street below, "Hello, all you cute guys!"

Kara sprang to the window and slammed it shut. "Brooke, how much coffee have you had?"

I giggled. "I'm just so over being the good, studious girl with the perfect GPA, bound for law school. That's Dad's dream." I twirled circles on our new shag rug with my toes. "I feel free to finally make up my own mind about my choices. I'm ready to start the next chapter of my life!"

2

"Kara, it's seven forty-five in the morning and blazing hot! Who in the world mandates classes begin mid-August in Austin, Texas? I'll be drenched in sweat before I even make it to my first class."

The word *sweat* made me think of Grandma Conrad's favorite reprimand, "Horses sweat; ladies glow." I looked at Kara to make sure she was listening. "Seriously, I'm gunna be a human firefly by the time I get to class."

Kara rolled her eyes then studied her class schedule.

I picked up my schedule. "How hard can this be? I've already placed out of the core courses, so these are just basic prerequisites."

As I flipped the pages of the schedule like a fan, a gust of wind ripped it out of my hand, sending it flying across the campus lawn. I lunged to grab it, only to be frustrated by another gust of wind that hiked my papers another couple of feet away. I hadn't memorized the stinkin' schedule, so I had to dive after it again. Desperate for "third time's a charm," I stomped on it before another gust threatened. I looked over at Kara, who was doubled over laughing.

I felt my face grow hot. "And you call yourself my best friend?"

She covered her mouth with her hand and squeaked, "Sorry."

We found a bench at the quad and examined the UT map to plot our class locations.

Kara stood. "Okay, I know how to get to my eight o'clock class. I'd better go, or I'll be late. See ya later."

"Yeah, see you back at the dorm." I watched Kara stride away in her T-shirt and tennis shoes. Other girls decked out in frilly tops, denim skirts, and pointed-toe flats were heading in the same direction. My friend clearly needed to update her wardrobe from high school geek to college chic. I didn't have to look down at what I was wearing to know I had no room to talk. How did we get through sorority rush dressed like this?

Rush week was finally over. Kara and I had pledged Tri Delt, Abbey's sorority. Was there ever any doubt I'd get in, with Abbey being Tri Delt sorority treasurer? Abbey's reaction to my acceptance seemed a little evasive. Knowing her, she was probably concerned I'd embarrass her.

Abbey was immersed in sorority and campus activities. Well, that is, until she flipped head-over-heels for her boyfriend, John Townsend. After that, I think she considered everything and everyone, other than John, a distraction and an annoyance. That included me.

I still thought her connections would help me get a strong college start. UT was such a huge campus, if I didn't take advantage of her connections, I'd remain unnoticed. I was hoping I could step out from behind Abbey's shadow when she graduated in the spring. Probably just wishful thinking.

My thoughts shifted as a guy plopped down at the end of the bench. Trying to be nonchalant, I sneaked a sidelong glance. I couldn't help noticing how cute he was as he scrolled through his phone. What guy could pull off looking like he was ready to catch the next beach wave with thick, almost too long, sandy hair and a muscular build yet appear as if he was going to run for congress, with his blue university striped Oxford shirt and khakis?

He must have sensed my gaze because he turned to me. "Hey."

His eyes! Bright emerald green! I felt my face heating up. I was sure the tell-tale sign of blotches consumed my fair cheeks. *C'mon, Brooke, say something!*

I blurted, "Hey!" I tucked my hair behind my ears.

He nodded at the campus map I was holding. "Looks like you're trying to figure out where your classes are. Are you new here?"

I attempted a smile, struggling to move my lips to form one. "Yeah, I'm a freshman." Ugh! I sounded like an idiot!

He smirked. "Well, I've been here for several years. I can show you to your first class if you'd like."

Yes! Absolutely! Yes! I collected myself and tried to sound casual. "Sure, that'd be all right. I need to go to Waggener Hall."

I pulled the zipper of my backpack to load my supplies, but it wouldn't budge. I tried again. It was stuck. Another thing I needed to update from high school. I flung the useless thing over my shoulder and picked up my books and spirals.

Carrying a stainless-steel mug and flaunting leather loafers, he walked with a smooth stride. "So, my name's Nathan. What's yours?"

"Brooke." Feeling awkward and uneasy, I juggled my books and spirals. Why didn't Abbey warn me about buying what seemed like a gazillion spirals?

Nathan looked down at me and chuckled. "Where are you from?"

I finally managed to balance my books. "Dallas."

He cocked his head. "Oh? I have an uncle who lives near Dallas. What part of Dallas?"

"University Park."

Nathan half-smiled and gave me a side glance. "Ah, a little rich girl, huh?"

I narrowed my eyes. Wow! I didn't like his superior tone. I picked up on a possible materialistic attitude. Wasn't sure what to do with that, so I gave him an Abbey look: inspecting his loafers then his eyes. "Where are you from?"

"From Conroe, north of Houston." He eased his Ray-Bans over his eyes.

I spotted the fraternity emblem on his stainless-steel mug then quickly looked away, not wanting him to notice I was interested in what fraternity it signified. He might think I was interested in him, which, of course, I was.

Apparently, he did notice because within seconds he asked, "Did you go through rush?"

"Yeah, I pledged Tri Delt."

I looked away, hoping to shut down further questioning that could reveal my sister was the reason I was accepted into Tri Delts. Why was it that everyone seemed to think it important that (A) you were Greek and (B) you pledged a "good" sorority? I got that it was a way to connect on a big campus. At least, that's what Mom and Abbey seemed to think. But how could a sorority define my identity?

Nathan interrupted my thoughts. "Hey! My fraternity is planning a mixer with the Tri Delts for Saturday night."

As he rattled on about his fraternity and their reputation for fun parties, I tried to hide my excitement about seeing him again by feigning calm. "Oh? That's cool."

He grinned. I wondered how well I'd pulled off calm.

We arrived at Waggener Hall, the building I had already mapped out, never really needing Nathan's guided escort.

"Thank you for your help."

His eyes held mine. His voice lowered. "I'll see you at the mixer Saturday night."

I replied in a pitch just below a squeal. "Yeah, I look forward to it."

I spun toward the massive building to head inside for class. I turned back to look at Nathan and noticed he smiled with what seemed like pleasure in his eyes. I squinted, trying to read the intent behind that frozen smile, which he maintained while slowly turning to walk away. He was incredibly good-looking. I wondered how many other girls had thought the same thing.

"Oh, I'm so glad to hear your first day of classes went well. I just spoke to Abbey and her classes were good too. I sent you a care package in the mail, sweetheart, so let me know when you get it. Love you, Brooke."

"Okay, Mom. I will. Love you too."

As soon as we'd hung up, my phone buzzed again. No surprise it was Abbey calling to see if I wanted to go shopping. It was obvious Mom had put her up to it.

But I jumped at the chance since I had no car. Dad had made me leave my car at home. His words still reverberated in my ears like a gong: "Abbey didn't have a car her first semester, so it's only fair. Anyway, it's one less thing for me to worry about, Brooke. You can focus on your studies, and I won't have to worry about you getting in a wreck. I know you're a good driver. It's the other drivers on the road I don't trust."

At the time, I wanted to say, "Okay, Dad, got it!"

Abbey picked me up, and we headed to the mall. She gripped the top of the steering wheel with her right hand, her extended right arm forming a barrier between us. From my high school debate training, I was able to analyze her body language, which screamed, "I don't want to be here with you."

"Brooke, I only have one hour to shop because I have plans with John." I nodded. "Of course."

Abbey had met John the previous year when he was a member of The Silver Spurs, the guys selected to take care of UT's longhorn mascot. Abbey was nominated Silver Spur Sweetheart, a pretty big deal.

As I enrolled at UT, John entered UT Law School. Since Dad had graduated from UT Law, he and John had hit it off the moment they met. Mom and I liked John right away too. He was goal-oriented yet laid-back, a great combination of attributes to have if you were going to spend time with Abbey.

On our shopping trip, Abbey and I hit three stores in the mall—the fastest shopping spree ever known to womankind, at least to women who like to shop.

During our drive back to the dorm, I broke the silence. "I met a really cute guy on campus. He walked me to my first class. The only thing was, the zipper of my backpack broke and I felt super awkward juggling my massive load of books and spirals."

Abbey tossed me a look. "Why didn't he offer to carry your books?" My sister made a good point, so I just shrugged.

Abbey pulled up to my dorm. "I'll pick up you and Kara for the mixer at seven o'clock Saturday night. Be on time."

She sped away to spend time with John. Saturday was their first dating anniversary, and she had filled a gift box with his favorites: chocolate chip cookies, a Silver Spurs alumni golf hat, and an iPod mini. I was certain she resented having to take us to the mixer rather than celebrate with John.

⬦

Entering my dorm room, I found Kara sitting at her desk, her books sprawled around her. "Kara, I wish you could have come shopping with Abbey and me! We found some cute tops, and I bought some UGGs."

Kara's smile spread across her lips, then both dimples appeared. "You were sweet to invite me, Brooke, and even be willing to wait 'til I finished classes, but I knew I'd be exhausted. The last thing I wanted was more walking. My feet are killing me."

It was no surprise she'd excluded Abbey from being willing to wait for her. Having been around my sister for years, Kara knew Abbey would never gladly wait for anyone.

Kara was much more focused on school success than shopping sprees anyway. She had taken a heavy class schedule, twenty-one credit hours. She was pre-med and had a long haul ahead of her.

She straightened her slumped shoulders. "I met a nice guy today in biochemistry. He's pre-med too."

I tilted my head. "That's awesome." I shot her bug eyes. "Maybe he can be your study buddy through med school." I winked.

Kara laughed, kicked off her shoes, and flung herself across the bed. "It's so like you to plan things to a T!" She smirked. "Sounds like you have my next eight years mapped out. How'd your day go?"

"Well, I met a frat guy, and he walked me to my first class. He's incredibly cute, and he'll be at our mixer Saturday night. He might be a little full of himself, though. I'll introduce you to him so you can tell me what you think."

"You know I'll give you my opinion." Kara grinned, exposing both dimples, then pointed to a box on the floor. "Amazon delivered our boxing gloves for the mixer. Yours are the gold gloves and mine the pink, right?"

"Yeah." I lunged to the box and opened it.

The theme of Nathan's fraternity mixer was a boxer bash. We planned to wear our cutest workout clothes to coordinate with the boxing gloves.

I examined my gloves. "I think these will go with my black Under Armour leggings. The gloves are gonna make for some great party pictures."

Relaxing on our beds, Kara and I talked about our classes. "Kara, I'm worried about my World Religion class. The professor seemed fixated on a kind of New Age theory. I want to be up on other religious beliefs—that's why I took the class. But I'm concerned about his lecture today."

I sat up on the side of my bed. "He suggested that Jesus was simply a prophet and good teacher. Of course, I shouldn't be so naïve as to assume that a professor of a world religion class would have a personal relationship with Jesus. He likely wouldn't. But today, I wanted to shout across the auditorium, 'Jesus is so much more!' I'm thinking that wouldn't have gone well."

Kara furrowed her brows. "That's tough. Your prof could give you a failing grade on your assignments if you don't show tolerance for all religious views."

"Yep, I'm afraid you're right." I sighed. "Kara, you know me. I've attended church most of my life, even memorized some Bible verses. But today, I was bothered that I've never studied the Bible for myself. I know Mom is into it and that probably brings her comfort. She's super involved in that women's Bible study. I've always thought I'd get into a Bible study when I get old like her." I grabbed my water bottle from my bedside table and took a swig. "But now that this prof is challenging my beliefs, I think I need to learn how to defend scriptural truths, like how you and I prepared for debates in high school."

Kara sat up half-way on her elbow and gazed out the window.

I opened a bag of chips and offered them to Kara. "Today's first day of classes was like rush week on steroids. Maddi made rush week so much easier than it probably would have been."

Kara poured some chips into a bowl and returned the bag. "Yeah. You're fortunate to have Maddi as your sorority big sis. Maddi is one of the sweetest sorority girls we've gotten to know."

I nodded. I first met Maddi when I had visited Abbey on campus last spring. She took the time to listen to Kara and me, making us feel like we mattered. She had something special, almost peaceful, about her. I hoped to ask Maddi if I could catch a ride with her next Sunday to her campus church.

Kara's big sister in the sorority was Abbey. Only natural, since they'd known each other for almost ten years.

Before I could get a chip into my mouth, my stomach growled so loudly, we both laughed. My laugh turned into a snort, which made us laugh even louder.

"Guess that's our call for supper." I snorted on purpose, imitating a pig.

As we walked to the dining hall, Kara's flip flops slapped in a slow, rhythmic pace. I slowed my steps to match hers.

She sighed. "I don't know about you, but I'm going to bed early tonight. It's been a full day and the week has only just begun."

3

Saturday night finally arrived, the night I'd been anticipating all week. Abbey pulled up to the dorm at seven o'clock sharp. Punctual as usual.

Since meeting Nathan, I'd been excited with the expectation of seeing him again. Yet when it was time to leave for the party, I became jittery—a complete basket case. Would Nathan remember me? Acknowledge my presence? Who was I kidding? He probably already had a girlfriend.

Kara and I piled into Abbey's car and barely got our doors closed before she sped off. I hurriedly buckled my seat belt as we zipped down the road. I glanced back to see Kara gripping the armrest.

I cleared my throat. "Abbey, do you remember that guy I told you about? The one who walked me to class Monday?"

Abbey sucked her teeth. "Vaguely. What's his name?"

"Nathan."

"Nathan who?"

"I didn't catch his last name."

Abbey rolled her eyes. "Then I wouldn't know. There are a lot of Nathans on campus."

Kara squirmed in the backseat. I'm sure she was uncomfortable with our sisterly discord.

Earlier that day, Kara and I had worked out at the gym then returned to the dorm to shower and use the facial masks I'd picked up at Ulta during my shopping whirlwind with Abbey. I fixed my hair in a ponytail and Kara put hers in a bun on top of her head. We wanted to look cute but still look like kickboxers. I never wore makeup when I worked out, but I wore it that night. I wanted to look my best for the boxer bash.

We arrived at the fraternity house. Shrubs that were manicured in the shapes of balls and cubes bordered the walkway leading to the massive front door. As we crossed the posh entryway, the first thing I noticed was what looked like a huge boxing ring, which was actually a dance floor. There were punching bags suspended by colorful strings of lights hanging from the ceiling. These fraternity guys must have paid a party decorator big bucks to come up with all of this. It was impressive.

The DJ was playing a blaring rendition of UT's fight song. A group of my sorority sisters, geared up in their colorful boxing gloves and workout clothes, sang at the top of their lungs with a bunch of the fraternity guys. The party photographer circulated, capturing candid shots.

I flinched when a hand rested on the small of my back. An electric bolt shot up my spine. I spun around to find Nathan standing so close, he was practically breathing in my hair. In all fairness, he probably hovered close to make sure I could hear him over the loud music. "Hey, Brooke. Glad to see you." His minty breath lingered.

I smiled and felt my face grow warm. I hated that I blushed so easily. I couldn't believe that he remembered my name! "Oh, hi, Nathan! Uh, I'd like for you to meet my roommate, Kara Williamson. Kara, this is Nathan . . ."

Nathan saved me, "Everett. Nathan Everett. Nice to meet you, Kara." They exchanged smiles and Nathan introduced Kara to Blake, a fraternity brother.

As the three of them engaged in small talk, I cast a glance around the room, searching for Abbey so that I could introduce her to Nathan. I finally spotted her scowling at me. Her face had disgust written all over it, lips pursed and nostrils flaring, reminding me of Mom's face the night I broke curfew.

I looked from Nathan to Kara. "Please excuse me for a moment." Kara gave me that look I knew so well. It implied, *Really? Are you bailing on me right now?* I flashed her a smile and tipped my head toward Abbey. My eyes met Nathan's. "I'll be right back."

I dodged several people in making my way to Abbey. "What's wrong, Abbey? Why are you looking at me like that?"

"Who's the guy whispering in your ear?" my gorgeous, sweet-as-pie sister hissed.

I was a little taken aback by her snake-like tone. "It's Nathan Everett, the guy I told you about. You know, the one who walked me to class Monday." Glad he had just clued me in on his last name so I wouldn't appear inept again.

She pulled me aside. "His reputation precedes him, and not in a good way. Be careful, Brooke. I'm not sure about him."

It was like she had sucker punched me.

Abbey wasn't done. "John called. Since it's our first dating anniversary, he wants to meet me at our favorite restaurant on Congress Street. I've arranged a ride back to the dorm for you and Kara with our sorority sister, Carissa. I would have asked Maddi, but she's not here yet." Abbey shot a quick glance toward the entrance, probably searching for Maddi's arrival. "Carissa offered when she overheard snippets of my phone conversation with John."

Carissa, a senior who was on track to graduate with Abbey and Maddi, was making her way back from the bar with a guy. Their arms were entwined.

"Hey, Carissa, thanks for offering to take Kara and me to our dorm later."

I wondered how she managed to keep her stringy strands of hair from getting stuck to her shiny pink lip gloss. She flipped her hair over her shoulder. Aha! That's how.

"No problem. Just let me know when you're ready to go." She flashed me a courtesy smile with her blinding pink lips while her guy steered her like a sailboat toward the dancefloor.

Abbey gripped my upper arms and looked me dead in the eye. "I'll call you tomorrow." In a hushed tone, she added, "Be careful. Remember what I said about Nathan. Stick close to Kara and Maddi." Abbey glanced around the room, radiating a photographic smile to others. Her smile flipped to a frown when her eyes darted back at me.

What drama! I refrained from rolling my eyes and simply nodded.

Abbey moved toward the door at the same time Maddi entered

the house. Petite Maddi was dwarfed in the grand entryway. Spotting Maddi, Abbey's shoulders fell, and her arms dropped loosely to her side. She stopped to talk to Maddi, who nodded then scanned the crowd until she saw me. Maddi and I exchanged smiles. Abbey glared at me with her sister-vampire-witch warning then left to meet up with John.

I scurried back to Nathan, who seemed to ignore the others as his gaze locked on me. Because of his *The Thinker* pose, I guessed he was wondering about that whole dramatic scene between my sister and me.

"So . . . I saw you talking with Abbey Conrad. Is she your sorority big sister?"

It was no surprise that Nathan knew Abbey's name. With all the campus organizations Abbey was involved in, lots of people knew her name. I could have just left Nathan with the impression that Abbey was my sorority big sister. That way he wouldn't conclude that the Tri Delts accepted me because of my family ties.

But really? How dishonest. And anyway, I was hoping this relationship would go somewhere. If it did, he'd eventually find out that Abbey and I were siblings. I fessed up, "No, she's my real sister. We're family."

I braced myself for a rude comment like, "Oh, so that's how you got into Tri Delts."

But without missing a beat, Nathan smiled. "I can see the resemblance. You're both beautiful."

My heart leaped. I searched his eyes for signs of mocking, but I saw none. Usually, I overheard comments like, "Abbey is gorgeous and, well, Brooke is cute." This was the first time someone, other than Mom, had ever told me I was beautiful.

I looked down at the floor, and it took me a couple of tries to find my voice. "Thanks."

"My pleasure. Would you like a soda or water?"

By his choice, I was sure he inferred I wasn't twenty-one after my airhead "I'm a freshman" announcement at our first encounter. "Um, water, please."

He disappeared to the bar and returned holding two glasses of water embellished with lime slices. At least I assumed his was also water.

He led me to a pub table and set our glasses down. "I'm a business marketing major and the fraternity's rush chairman."

Hmm, reasons why he was such a great conversationalist?

He nudged my glass toward me. "I plan to graduate in the spring."

"Brooke! I'm so glad to see you made it to the mixer!" I broke my gaze on Nathan to see Maddi standing at our table.

"Oh, Maddi. I'd like to introduce you to Nathan Everett. Nathan, this is Maddi Simms."

"It's nice to meet you, Maddi."

"Hello, Nathan. Then she squinted. "Have we had a class together? You look familiar."

Nathan smiled, showing his perfectly aligned white teeth. "No, I don't think so."

Madi half-smiled. "Yeah, who knows." She turned toward me, glancing down at the lime slice perched on my glass. "Carissa left with her date, so I'll drive you and Kara to your dorm whenever you're ready."

"I'd be glad to take them back to their dorm." Nathan shifted his body toward me, resting his forearm on the tabletop.

Maddi stood tall . . . as much as her five-foot-one height would allow. She raised her chin. "No, I'll take them to the dorm. It's good to know you, Nathan." She glared at him for several seconds before spinning to face me, knocking over my glass. Water spilled over the table and dribbled onto the floor.

"Oh! I apologize, Brooke. How clumsy of me. Here, take my bottled water. I haven't even opened it yet," she said, as she mopped the spill with the stack of table napkins. Finishing the job, she looked up at me. "I'll keep an eye out to see when you and Kara are ready to leave." She smiled, but it didn't reach her eyes. I got her message.

Once she'd left to mingle with others, Nathan lifted the corners of his mouth into a smirk. "Wow, she wasn't backing down." He slowly shook his head. "For such a tiny gal, she's pretty authoritative."

Determined to defend Maddi's integrity and loyalty, I said, "She's my sorority big sis and the sorority president, so she's just watching out for me."

Nathan stared at me, his eyes piercing, until he blinked. He flashed a smile and extended his hand. "Would you like to dance?"

"Sure!"

He grabbed my hand and pulled me close as we zig-zagged around the dance floor, trying to find an open spot. It was hard to find one, not just because the dance floor was packed, but because we were forced to dodge couples who were dancing while holding splashing cocktails.

It was no surprise that Nathan was an amazing dancer. As the DJ transitioned from fast music to a slow Garth Brooks song, Nathan grinned and swung me close. Because he was probably six foot two, he had to crane his neck to look down at me with those emerald green eyes. He led my untrained steps with so much skill, I followed his lead as if I'd been dancing for years.

But I still felt awkward—like I needed to say something to break the silence between us. "I just love Garth Brooks's music."

"Yeah, he's great. Have you ever heard him in concert?"

I shook my head.

"Seriously? Aw, you've got to see him perform. He's coming to campus in a few months. I'll check to see if I can get us tickets. I'd like to take you, Brooke."

Had he just asked me out? He held me even closer. I was certain he could feel, even hear, my rapid heartbeat.

He whispered in my ear, "You smell so good."

I could hardly breathe. He skillfully twirled me out, then back close again. This guy! This was happening! I was literally dancing like I knew how to dance, and with the hottest guy on campus.

No matter what music played, we kept dancing. We paused only to get our photo taken together. That party photographer was sneaky! I was certain he captured my google eyes as I looked at Nathan with unabashed infatuation. I hoped that photo of my goofy expression wouldn't get posted on Facebook. Nathan guided me back to the dance floor and swung me around with ease. We no longer talked. Words seemed unnecessary, so we just danced.

When the DJ announced the last song of the evening, I thought I'd probably never hear from Nathan again. As if he'd read my mind, he tipped my chin up so that our eyes met. "I'd like to see you again. Can I call you tomorrow?"

I wanted to jump up to the ceiling with indescribable joy, but managed a normal tone. "Of course, I'd like that."

When the song ended, we programmed each other's contact information into our cell phones. Couples were leaving the dance floor. Girls were grabbing their purses. I turned to search the room for Kara, who I'd noticed earlier seemed to be having fun dancing with a bunch of different guys.

I felt Nathan's arms around me, and I stopped looking for Kara. He turned me to face him. "I hate to see you go. Which dorm do you live in?"

"Hardin House. Where do you live?"

He gave a short, half-suppressed laugh. "Here. Would you like a grand tour of the house?"

As if on cue, Maddi appeared. "I had the guys pull my car around to the front." Kara stood behind her. It was time to leave.

Nathan drew me close, lingering in the embrace. When he whispered, "Call you tomorrow," my face tingled. I nodded.

As I walked away, I turned to see him smiling with pleasure, like he'd just devoured the first course of a delicious meal. His smile remained frozen as he turned away, just as it had Monday morning. I was still perplexed by the motive behind that smile.

Driving to the dorm, Maddi asked what we thought of the party. Kara and I blabbered nonstop about the awesome DJ and incredible decorations. Maddi nodded, appearing to listen intently.

When there was finally a lull in our chatter, Maddi said, "Brooke, tell me about Nathan."

"Well, we met on campus Monday, and he walked me to class. He told me he'd see me at the mixer tonight, so I've been on pins and needles all week."

"Yep, I can vouch for that!" Kara interjected.

I snickered. "We barely got a chance to talk tonight, but dancing with him just—I don't' know—it just felt right."

"Do you think you'll see him again?" She kept her eyes on the road.

"I'd like to, but I have no idea. He said he'd call me. But who knows?"

Maddi took her eyes off the road momentarily and peered at me. "God knows, and He has just the right man planned for you when the time is right."

She didn't lecture me. Her words were gentle. I sensed that peace about her again.

After Maddi dropped us off and Kara and I were on the elevator, I realized I'd forgotten to ask Maddi for a ride to church. I could have called her at that moment, but I hadn't yet asked Kara if she'd like to go with us.

"Do you want to go to the campus church tomorrow? I've been thinking about asking Maddi if I could catch a ride with her."

"I'd like to go, but not tomorrow. I need to get some class work done before Monday."

I nodded. "Yeah, I need to study too." What a lie! My real reason was that I'd have to turn off my phone for church service and possibly miss Nathan's call. That was, if he really intended to follow through with his promise to call. What was I thinking? I wasn't in his league.

My ringing phone startled me. Seriously? Nathan calling? I yanked it out of my purse and flipped it open. Maddi's name appeared on the screen.

"Maddi."

"Hey, Brooke. I apologize that I neglected to offer you and Kara a ride to church tomorrow."

"That's so unreal because Kara and I were just talking about going. But we both decided we have too much studying to do tomorrow" Wow, another lie! "Maybe I can take you up on your offer for next Sunday?"

"Yes, absolutely! Have a good night."

"You too . . . and thanks, Maddi." She seemed confident, yet humble. I needed to hang out with her more.

4

The next day, I sat at my desk in my uncomfortable retro chair, tapping my pen. I was having a hard time concentrating. Kara put her headphones on. My cue to stop tapping. I couldn't stop thinking about Nathan. It was noon and he hadn't called. *Stop, Brooke!* I'd never been this pathetic over a guy, not even in high school.

I jumped when my phone rang, and grabbed it to look at the caller ID. Just Abbey. What was wrong with me? There was a time I'd have relished the opportunity to talk with my sister. Talk like her, walk like her, look like her, be like her. I punched *Accept*. "Hey."

"Hey, Brooke. I'm calling to make sure Carissa got y'all back to the dorm safely."

"Carissa left early, but Maddi stepped up and gave us a ride."

"Are you kidding me?"

Through her headphones, Kara must have heard Abbey's yelling because she looked at me with raised eyebrows.

"I can't believe Carissa bailed!"

I held my phone away from my ear.

Hopeful Abbey had finished her ranting, I said, "Listen, Carissa left after she made sure Maddi could take us back to the dorm. How is that any different from what you did?"

Silence on her end. Then, "Yeah, I guess you're right. Okay, well, glad y'all made it back safely."

"Yeah, thanks for calling."

"Wait. I'm also calling to find out if you heeded my warning to steer clear of Nathan."

"Nope. We danced together for the entire party, and I had the time of my life." Silence again.

"What is it, Abbey? Are you surprised that a good-looking senior could show interest in a dog-faced freshman, like me? That he approached me on campus and walked me to class? That he spent his entire time with me at the mixer? That he showed a genuine interest in me, complimented my looks, and made me feel special? Do you realize he's the only guy who has ever done that? In my life? No, you wouldn't because all those things are daily, mundane occurrences for you. You wouldn't know because you're too busy with John and your selfish ways to pay me any mind." I stopped to breathe.

I saw Kara staring at me with bulging eyes, her headphones dangling from her hand.

"Are you finished?" Abbey's pitch was slightly shrill. A pitch I'd never heard from her before.

"I'm not sure. What I am sure of is that I want a meaningful relationship with someone other than Mom, uh, oh and Kara." I grimaced at Kara and mouthed, "Sorry."

Kara shrugged and mouthed, "No problem."

"Okay, Brooke. Have it your way. Just know I'm a phone call away, and remember, I warned you."

After we hung up, I took a deep breath.

Kara took a deep breath too. "Whoa! Who are you?"

"Hopefully, I'm not Abbey's tag-along minion anymore." I cradled my face in the palms of my hands. "Kara, am I totally messed up? Am I becoming obsessed with dating? With Nathan?"

"I think we both need to be careful about looking to other people for our happiness. People have way too many faults and weaknesses to be depended on in that way."

"How old are you? Ninety?"

"I'm not old enough to know much, yet I'm not getting any younger either, especially with my research paper due tomorrow. Unlike you, I have to study to make an A." Kara stood up from her desk and shoved her books into her backpack. "I'm going to the library. You wanna come?"

"Thanks, Kara, but I think I'll stay here."

She heaved a long sigh, hoisted her backpack on, then scrambled to the door. "'K, see ya later."

I picked up my pen and resumed tapping. I couldn't believe how I'd just confronted Abbey. Usually, she was the leader with her authoritative attitude and I, the follower. There was a huge difference in our looks, too. Abbey was a blonde, a salon-highlighted blonde, with striking blue eyes, and a radiant complexion. I was a mousey-blondish brunette with narrow eyes and acne. My dermatologist said it wasn't acne, just hormones. I just avoided magnifying mirrors.

Despite our differences, when Abbey and I were little, we stuck together like gum on a shoe because our parents worked around the clock—Mom with her counseling practice, and Dad with his law firm. We had a strict nanny who never smiled and wouldn't even let us watch *Little Mermaid* because she claimed it was filled with satanic messages. We were relieved when Dad's law firm flourished in size and revenue and Mom became a stay-at-home mom, letting Nazi Nanny go. Mom let us watch *Little Mermaid* as much as we wanted while she cleaned the house obsessively. So strange that she was a professional counselor who turned neurotic over housekeeping.

About the time Abbey was in ninth grade and I was in sixth, Mom started reading the Bible and paying more attention to us and less to how the house looked. She said that the more she read, the more she yearned to discover the fullness of God's redemptive plan. She even joined a women's Bible study.

I looked at my phone. *Nothing.* I stared at my opened textbook. *Concentrate!*

It was almost four-thirty when my phone finally lit up and I saw Nathan's name on the screen. A jolt shot through me. I grabbed the phone then paused, allowing it to ring several more times. *Be cool, Brooke. Don't mess this up.* I tried to answer like it was a sales call. "Hello?"

"Hi, Brooke. I've been at the library all day. I have a major exam coming up. But the whole time I studied. . .I couldn't stop thinking about you."

Stay calm! I worked at slowing my breathing. "Nathan! Glad to hear from you. The mixer was really fun last night."

"Dancing with you was incredible. Last night, we really connected. I was wondering if you're available tomorrow night for dinner. I'd like to take you to Salt Lick Barbecue out in the Hill Country. They have the best barbecue around."

Oh! Wow! "Yes, of course."

"Seriously, I can't wait to see you again. I'll pick you up at six, then?" I agreed and we said goodbye.

Once I hung up, I squealed in both shock and frenzy. I had a date with the cutest guy on campus! I'm pretty sure I screamed way too loudly because Kara burst into the room. "What in the world! Brooke, are you okay?"

She'd just returned from the library and had undoubtedly heard me from the elevator. I giggled then blurted, "Yes! Guess who just asked me out!"

She paused before answering. "Nathan?"

I nodded frantically and I was certain I grinned from ear to ear. I waited for her reciprocal excitement, but she only stood stone-faced.

Kara looked down at the floor, fidgeting with her backpack straps.

Finally, she looked up, her eyebrows forming a deep V. "Uh, I feel like I need to tell you, um, I saw Nathan today behind a study carrel in a corner of the library. I started to walk around it to say hi but stopped when I saw he was with a girl. He had his hands all over her and was whispering in her ear. She had her eyes closed and was giggling."

Kara shifted her weight. "Neither of them saw me, so I was able to slip away unnoticed to another area of the library. Brooke, I'm so sorry, but I think Nathan is a player."

I felt like I'd been punched in the gut. His words, "I couldn't stop thinking about you" flooded my mind. What a liar!

I blinked, breathed in, picked up my phone, and punched *Recents.* Nathan answered, "Hey, beautiful!"

Another lie! I gripped the phone. My breathing deepened. My voice trembled. "Hey, I'm not going be able to go with you tomorrow night. I just realized I'm not available."

There was silence on his end. I started to hang up. Then he spoke. "What's that supposed to mean? A minute ago, you were glad to go out with me. Now you're 'not available'?"

"Yeah, that's right." I punched *End* and threw the phone onto the bed.

I breathed in, held my breath, and let it out slowly.

Kara didn't move. Her mouth agape.

My phone lit up with Nathan's name as the caller. I grabbed it and hit *Decline*.

Kara dropped her backpack, crossed the room, and hugged me.

I reflected on Nathan's lie. "He'd claimed he was studying for a major exam, couldn't stop thinking about me!" I tasted the saltiness of my tears and swiped them away. "It's not like we were exclusive. I have to admit, Abbey warned me about him."

Kara stepped back and looked at me with watery eyes. "I'm sorry it turned out this way."

I breathed out a mirthless half-laugh, tears streaming down my face. "Yeah, me too."

5

Monday mornings were rough enough, but this morning looked especially grim as I peered out my window at the threatening rainclouds. I needed to get going if I was to make it to my nine o'clock class on time. I never fully concentrated yesterday on the assigned readings for my World Religion class, or any other class for that matter. I hadn't slept well, so I decided to stop by Starbucks on the way.

I headed out in my cute Burberry rain boots, a definite perk to this dreary morning. I quickened my steps as occasional rain droplets turned into massive thuds, pelting sideways. I ducked into Starbucks before I was completely soaked. Once I had sweet coffee in hand, my momentum picked up and my optimism soared. I was hopeful I might just make it on time.

That was until I saw Nathan leaning against the arched entrance of Waggener Hall looking down at his phone. He looked sleek in his waterproof golf jacket and cap. I stopped dead in my tracks. I knew my hair must have looked like I felt—a frazzled mess. What was he doing here? How was I supposed to deal with this?

He looked up from his phone and spotted me approaching. As I neared the entrance, he spoke in his low, smooth tone that resonated deep inside me. "Hello, Brooke. I remembered you had class here and, well, your call last night puzzled me." He cocked his head to one side. "You sounded upset. Are you all right?"

I seriously had to figure out what to say to this guy. Rushing passers-by turned their heads toward us, some doing double takes. I didn't blame them. After all, who stands around talking in the pouring rain?

The coffee that had tasted sweet and comforting five minutes ago churned in my stomach. I shifted my weight and squeezed my coffee cup. "Yeah, I'm fine. I, uh, have a lot going on. Maybe I'll see you around sometime."

I pulled the door open and entered the building. This time, I didn't look back.

I'm guessing Kara spoke to Abbey about the crazy emotional roller coaster I rode yesterday because, later that night, Abbey and Maddi took Kara and me out for dinner at a trendy Mexican restaurant. The sounds of mariachi music and the smell of freshly baked tortillas indicated that this place was the real deal.

We gorged ourselves on the best Mexican food this side of the border while laughing at Abbey's and Maddi's hilarious sorority antics. I didn't bring up my earlier rain-drenched encounter with Nathan. I didn't want to ruin our fun.

Abbey was asking the waiter for the check when I noticed Kara's eyes widen with alarm as she stared past me.

"Kara, what?" I started to turn to see what captured her attention.

Kara kicked me under the table. "Don't turn around!"

I turned anyway. It took me no more than a second to see. I gulped.

Nathan was at the restaurant entrance with his arm around a very attractive, tall blonde. If she wasn't a model, she could've been. But the natural kind—not much make-up or fuss. She gazed dreamily into Nathan's green eyes with her brilliant blues. Nathan's polished dental smile made him look as if he'd just won the lottery. He led his beauty to the hostess, who proceeded to seat them.

I slowly turned back around. Maddi extended her hand to cover mine.

"Just yesterday, he asked me out for tonight. Wow, he moves fast," I whispered.

Once Abbey had settled the bill, we silently got up to leave. As I walked, I kept my eyes focused on the exit door. Exiting was my escape. I didn't want to set eyes on him again.

Driving to the sorority house to drop off Maddi, I broke the heavy silence in the car. "I was glad y'all were with me tonight when I saw Nathan, with his arm wrapped all over that girl."

Staring out the window into the darkness, illuminated only by an occasional streetlight, I breathed in slowly.

Abbey reached across and patted my arm. "I've heard he looks for freshmen girls to lead them on, with the sole purpose of getting them into bed."

Maddi's voice resonated softly from the back seat. "Yeah, I met Nathan in a public speaking class two years ago. Then, last year, I tried my best to console two sweet freshmen girls, one in February and the other in March. Both came crying to me because Nathan had suddenly dumped them for another girl. Neither of them understood why. At the time, I suspected he had impure motives."

"I'm sickened by the thought of him; completely disgusted." I heaved in another deep breath. "Y'all, I seriously want to slap him into next year."

Abbey snickered. "You sound like Grandma Conrad. Although she would have used the correct expression, 'slap him into the middle of next week' . . . just say'n."

I sighed audibly, not in the mood at that moment to tolerate my sister's corrections. "Yes, I know, Abbey. But next week isn't far enough for Nathan. I clearly want to slap him into next year."

That must have been the comic relief everyone needed because the car was suddenly blasted with laughter.

When our laughter died down, Maddi spoke. "Since we're not sure to what extent the rumors are true, I think it best, for now, that we pray for him and all girls in his path. Remember Romans twelve nineteen: 'Beloved, never avenge yourselves, but leave it to the wrath of God.'"

I wanted to laugh out loud again but wouldn't dare offend Maddi. It was kinda funny, though, how Maddi, so tiny and spunky, reminded me of a little old grandma with her pearls of wisdom. Not at all like my grandma Conrad, whose "words of wisdom" were abrasive in every way. Maddi's wisdom was different . . . truly heartfelt and well-meaning.

We arrived at the sorority house, and before Maddi opened the car door to get out, I thanked her for being such a true friend.

As Abbey drove us to our dorm, she looked deep in thought. Finally, she said, "Sis, I thank God for His protection over you and His provision in our lives. I regret that I've neglected you in my busyness, and, well, God is convicting me. Forgive me. I'll try to be a better sister and be available for you. Are you okay?"

Did my sister just apologize to me? "Yeah, I'll be fine. I'm thankful that I didn't get caught up in Nathan's deceit. Now, I just need to somehow forgive him. Also, feel free to say, 'I told you so.'"

"I hope you don't think I would actually say those words. I was in your shoes not so long ago and Maddi could have said, 'I told you so,' but didn't. True friends and sisters are a gift never to be taken for granted."

We pulled up to the dorm and before Kara and I got out, Abbey had something more to say. "Let's ask God to help us all forgive Nathan." She led us in prayer.

When we got back to our room, Kara spoke just above a whisper. "The girl who was with Nathan at the restaurant tonight was the same girl he was with at the library yesterday."

I crossed my arms around my waist. "To make matters even worse, she lives in this dorm."

Kara sat on her bed, placing her palms on her thighs and straightening her back. "Yeah, I've seen her in the dining hall."

I had a sick feeling in the pit of my stomach, and it wasn't the tacos. "I keep reminding myself that Nathan and I were never exclusive. In college, most people date different people—no big deal." I began washing my face. "Come to think of it, that was what I wanted when I came here, to date different guys. But nice guys! This guy, Nathan— what a deceiver. He's not to be trusted."

Once I'd changed into my pajamas, I plopped on my bed. "I'm gunna stop being naïve when it comes to smooth-talking guys, especially if their interests seem sketchy. From now on, I'm guarding my heart."

Kara leaned back onto her elbows. "Please don't guard your heart to the extent that you miss out on the relationships that God intends for you."

"Yeah, you're right, Kara. Thank you for always having my back. I'm going to bed. I'm exhausted."

As I lay in bed, I closed my eyes and silently asked God to help me forgive Nathan. I couldn't remember the last time I'd initiated a prayer on my own. I knew, more than ever before, that I needed God in my life.

6

"Wake up, Kara! It's game day!" I picked up the TV remote, turned to ESPN College Game Day, and pumped up the volume. Kara buried her head under her pillow.

It was the first Saturday of the football season. Later in the day, UT Longhorns would be playing Kansas State. My parents were already in town for the tailgate they'd be hosting on the lawns of the LBJ library. They were both UT alums, and this annual tailgate was the highlight of their football season.

For the game, Maddi had set me up with a blind date, a guy she knew from her church. His name was Mark and he was a KA pledge. I was excited that I would be sitting in the KA fraternity's fifty-yard line section at the game. Mark had called me several times just to talk. His major was architecture, and my sorority sisters told me that his dad was a renowned architect in the Austin area.

When Mark picked me up for the game, I could see he was far better looking than I'd imagined from our phone conversations with his strong jawline and broad shoulders. He stood tall in his blue jeans and boots. But there was no spark between us.

Mark and I approached the tailgate. Seeing Mom and Dad from a distance made me realize how much I'd missed them.

They'd arranged a barbecue cookout with a big screen that televised the pregame coverage. My parents were buried in a sea of burnt orange—the school color worn by all their alumni friends. I caught a glimpse of their faces peeking through the crowd, most likely searching for me.

As soon as they spotted me, they waved and walked briskly toward us. Following our hugs, I introduced them to Mark as my date for the evening. They seemed captivated with his polite demeanor. Even though I had no interest in dating Mark long-term, he'd be the perfect date, a true gentleman. That suited me just fine, especially after having dealt with Nathan's cruel dishonesty.

The barbecue had a savory aroma that drifted through the air, inviting us to feast. Mark and I jumped into the buffet line. Dad had been smoking barbecue at tailgates for as long as I could remember. Every bite that melted in my mouth brought back great memories of family times.

Huddled over his plate, Mark looked up and gave me a lopsided grin between bites. "Brooke, this is the best barbecue I've ever eaten. And what makes this mac'n'cheese so irresistible?"

I laughed. "Yep, everyone says that about our Southern Macaroni Pie. The secret is in the eggs and longhorn cheese—and, of course, the tons of butter."

After finishing off huge helpings, Mark and I said goodbye to my parents. Dad shook Mark's hand as I turned to Mom. "I'll see you at church in the morning at nine o'clock?"

Mom nodded several times in rapid succession. Reaching in for a hug, she whispered, "I hope you have a good time on your date. Mark seems like a nice young man."

Pretty sure Abbey had told her about the Nathan fiasco. "Yes, Mom. Mark's a really nice guy—and we're just friends."

Mom pulled away and grinned. "Gotcha. Dad and I look forward to seeing you in the morning, sweetheart. I love you."

"Love you too, Mom."

7

Bright and early the next morning, I received Maddi's text: *Ten minutes away.*

Kara and I rushed downstairs to grab a coffee in the lobby before heading outside the dorm to wait on a bench. I breathed in the aroma of the rich coffee. With every sip, its warmth permeated my body.

But I almost choked on it as a black BMW rolled to a stop, and Nathan's new blonde babe stepped out of the car. She wore gold stilettos and a cocktail dress, obviously from the night before. She lingered, talking to Nathan through the open passenger door. That's when I saw his gaze shift past her, straight at me. He had an irritatingly smug look on his face as he looked me up and down. I quickly averted my eyes, searching longingly down the street for Maddi's car.

The slamming of the passenger door was followed by the screeching of his tires. Once the blonde beauty disappeared into Hardin House, I leaned toward Kara. "I can't believe that just happened right in front of me. How can I be at the wrong place at the wrong time yet again?"

She eyed me. "Maybe you're at the right place at the right time as a confirmation that you escaped getting involved with Nathan. Did you see her? Her hair was in knots, and her face was smudged with mascara. They both looked pretty rough, maybe hung-over."

I nodded. I'd been blessed to have escaped Nathan's deception.

Just then, Maddi pulled up. We jumped into her car and headed for church.

"Maddi, we just saw Nathan dropping off his new girlfriend. I'm actually feeling relief that I didn't get involved with him."

Maddi's face lit up with a smile as she glanced my way. "I am so happy to hear you say that! How did your date go with Mark?"

"We had a fun time! Thanks for setting me up with such a nice, considerate guy."

"I knew he'd be a polite date. We may see him at church."

"No, he said today is his mom's birthday. He's joining his parents at their church in the hill country."

Arriving at the church, we met Mom, Dad, Abbey, and John. I sat next to Mom and took out my Bible. The church was studying the book of Luke. The pastor read Luke 6:37. "Judge not, and you will not be judged; condemn not, and you will not be condemned; forgive, and you will be forgiven."

I pondered the relationship between Nathan and his new girl. Who was I to judge that girl and, if I was honest, condemn Nathan? I had plenty of sinful ways of my own, being judgmental was only one.

The pastor read verse 41. "Why do you see the speck that is in your brother's eye, but do not notice the log that is in your own eye?"

I bowed my head and silently gave thanks to God for protecting me and reminding me of my need for Him and His forgiveness. When I looked up, Mom was glancing sideways at me.

After the church service, Mom and Dad treated us to brunch.

Mom and I got a chance to talk privately in the ladies' room, of all places. But really, it is the all-time best place for girl talk.

"How are you doing, sweetheart? Everything okay?"

I told her about my encounters with Nathan, including seeing him with the blonde. "The sermon today convicted me of my judgmental attitude."

Mom paused as she washed her hands. "What will you do in response to the Bible message?"

"Well, I've asked God to forgive me for judging Nathan and his new girlfriend. I've also prayed that God will help me, in turn, to forgive them."

Mom's eyes, accentuated with crow's feet, lit up as she smiled. "Then God forgives you. Now, maybe you can show an act of kindness? You say the girl lives at Hardin House. What do you think about seeking her out to befriend her? Do you remember how you were there for Kara when she lost her mom? You might become a source of support for this girl also."

I stared at Mom, shocked. I couldn't believe what she was suggesting.

"But, Mom, what if she rejects me? What if she tells Nathan that I'm trying to be friends with her? That could blow up in my face. He'll assume I'm doing it with ulterior motives." I crossed my arms around my waist.

Mom tossed her hand towel into the bin and gently touched my elbows. "Well, sweetheart, even Jesus, who was perfect, suffered people's rejections and false accusations. But in Luke chapter six verse thirty-five, Jesus, knowing He'd be persecuted, told us to love our enemies. I think you should pray about it; that God would provide opportunities for you to get to know this girl. And, most important, that God would be glorified through it all."

I hugged Mom and said a silent prayer of thanksgiving for her.

When we returned to the table, the waitress was serving our food. Dad furrowed his brows, creating deep lines resembling railroad tracks on his forehead. He whispered something to Mom, and she responded with a smile and a nod.

I assumed their exchange was about our long time in the ladies' room, which amused me. Dad probably worried that when we didn't return right away, one of us got sick to our stomachs. I was certain he didn't have a clue that Mom and I were having a heart-to-heart. His suppositions were usually more logical than emotional.

I was grateful that, no matter how old I was, my parents never stopped caring for me.

8

By the first of October, Kara and I had been going to church with Maddi for several weeks. We'd gotten to know the lead pastor, David, and his family. We'd also started going to one of the church's community groups for single adults and married couples that met on Thursday nights.

We met in the home of a young couple, Michael and Caroline Pate, who had two adorable pre-school children. Toys and Cheerio snack cups littered the family room, making their beautiful house feel like a home. Michael was a police sergeant and Caroline, a part-time accountant. They were such gracious hosts who navigated the Bible studies in ways that always facilitated great group interaction.

When Abbey asked John to go with her to community group, he agreed, but hesitantly. "You know, Ab, I hate group studies like that. I'll go, but I'm not going to talk."

"You're not going to talk, even though you're preparing to be a lawyer. What a disconnect."

"Communicating law in a courtroom is totally different than sitting around talking about the Bible with a group of strangers. But, as I said, I'll go with you."

Thursday night, Michael welcomed them as they entered his home, shaking Abbey and John's hands. "Hello, I'm Michael Pate."

"I'm Abbey Conrad and this is my boyfriend, John Townsend."

It was a huge ice breaker when Michael responded, "Hey, we have another group member named John. I'll introduce you two. We can never have too many johns in the house." I watched John enjoy a full laugh and, at that moment, I knew he was in.

Abbey confided in me later that if John had turned down her invitation to join the group, she would have had to seriously reconsider their relationship. But despite the demands of law school, he carved out the time and became fully engaged.

"Was that old man in the pew behind us snoring or was that your stomach growling?"

"Thanks, Kara. Glad you think I sound like an old man. Why am I always so hungry?"

"Because you're hyper and burn a thousand calories a minute." She beamed a dimpled smile.

"Then let's go back to the dorm and indulge in the famous Hardin House Sunday brunch, the best meal of the week."

Kara and I left the church and walked to Hardin House. The long walk made me work up even more of an appetite for the buttered yeast rolls, which were to die for.

As we entered the dining room, the sweet aroma of freshly baked bread was enticing. Kara only had time to grab a sandwich-to-go since she was meeting up with the guy from her biochemistry class at the library.

Once we had our food, I saw Nathan's attractive girlfriend sitting alone at a table in the corner. Kara must have spotted her too because she whispered, "Here's your opportunity to reach out to her. I gotta go."

I scowled at Kara, hoping she'd read my mind: *Thanks for bailing on me.*

She grinned and mouthed, "Get over it," and hurried out of the dining room.

Remembering what Mom had suggested, I reluctantly approached the girl. "Okay if I join you?"

Half-smiling, she replied, "Sure."

I swept my tongue over my lips to moisten them. "I'm Brooke Conrad."

"Nice to meet you. I'm Leah Morris." She nodded toward the door. "Will your roommate be returning to join us?"

"No, she had to go to the library. How about yours?"

"She's with her boyfriend. She's at his place all the time."

Wow, what a contrast! My roommate was headed to the library and her roommate was living with the boyfriend. *Again, Lord, forgive me for my judgmental attitude.*

Leah took a sip of her tea. "I've seen you and your roommate in here several times." She shifted to the side as she crossed her legs.

I wondered if Kara and I seemed unapproachable those several times. "I'm from Dallas. Where are you from?"

"New York."

"New York! You're far from home."

She pressed her lips together.

Thinking she didn't want to talk about home, I changed the subject to school and found out she was a freshman and undecided about her major. We also talked about our sororities. Leah was a legacy—her mom and grandma had been in the same sorority in their college days.

Twirling her hair, she added, "I'd grown close to my grandma before she passed away last year. She moved from South Carolina to New York to live with my mom and me when Dad moved out and Mom was pretty much lost to depression. I'm not so close to my parents. They divorced when I was in junior high and Dad moved to California, where he started a new family. I've hardly seen him since."

I racked my brain in search of something comforting to say.

She looked down at her lap and scrunched her nose. "I apologize. I'm not sure why I just shared all of that with you. I guess it's that you're a good listener."

I'm usually the one who talks, not listens. I think this girl just spilled her guts because she's super lonely. "I'm sorry you lost your grandma. I felt my world was crashing down when I lost my grandpa. It was ten years ago, but I still miss him."

She looked up and studied me. She seemed to be searching my soul. "Thank you for empathizing."

As we talked, I noticed that Leah's complexion was pale and dark circles cupped her eyes—a stark contrast from when I saw her at the restaurant. That night, as she gazed up at Nathan, her face was radiant with blushing sunglows.

Of course, I never mentioned that I saw her that night or that I once had a major crush on Nathan. I hadn't seen them together since that Sunday morning in front of the dorm. I hoped her sorrow wasn't because he'd broken her heart.

Once we finished lunch, I invited Leah to grab a cup of coffee. "I'm addicted to coffee in the mornings and literally fly into Starbucks most days on the way to class. I have a nine o'clock tomorrow morning. Want to join me before class?"

She perked up. "Sure! I have a nine o'clock on Mondays as well."

"We could meet in the dorm lobby in the morning—around eight?"

"That'll work."

"Looking forward to seeing you in the morning, Leah."

"You too. I'm glad to have finally met you."

Walking away, my thoughts ricocheted. *Wow! The gorgeous girlfriend was glad she finally met . . . me? As far as outward appearances, she had it all. But inwardly, she seemed empty, unhappy, and so alone.*

9

I got to the lobby at eight o'clock the next morning. Leah was waiting for me. She looked adorable with her hair curled in soft waves around her face. As she approached, I hollered, "I'm ready for my Starbucks fix!" She laughed softly and we left the dorm, talking easily back and forth.

Before reaching Starbucks, Leah smoothed her blouse. "Thank you for introducing yourself yesterday. After you left, I started feeling guilty. Um, I should tell you that I already knew a bit about you before we met." She fidgeted with the loops of her long beaded necklace.

I swallowed hard, unsure I wanted to hear what she was having difficulty saying.

"I browsed the Greek party pictures online after meeting a really cute guy in August." She cleared her throat. "I wanted to find out more about him and if he was dating anyone. That's when I saw a photo of you and him at a party. I'd feel horrible if I messed things up between the two of you."

Please let this go well, God. I clasped my hands together. "Would that guy be Nathan?"

She gave me a side glance. "Yeah." Her voice was barely audible.

"Leah, it's all good." I flashed my palm in the air. "Promise."

We got to Starbucks and ordered. Then we settled at a table where we could wait for our names to be called.

Once seated, I took a moment to select my words. Straightening, I placed my folded hands on the table. "I never dated Nathan. I have to admit that I had a major crush on him, but it didn't last." I paused before asking, "Are y'all dating?"

Leah gave a slow blink and sat back in her chair. "We were. He abruptly stopped calling. Since then, I've seen him with another girl."

Hearing the sadness in her voice and seeing it in her eyes, I wanted to hug her. But people were shuffling all around us, and I didn't want to embarrass her.

The barista called our names. We grabbed our lattes, headed to the West Mall, and found a bench.

I leaned toward Leah, clutching my cup with both hands close to my chest. "I'm so sorry. If it helps at all, my sister warned me that Nathan has a bad reputation. You deserve better."

She studied me, the sapphire in her eyes glistening with moisture. "No, you don't know me. I'm broken in so many ways."

"You're no more broken than me or anyone else." I knew it was almost time for class, but I couldn't just leave her like this. I paused, then added, "Do you want to get together later?"

Her response was stalled and seemed measured. "Well, I have class 'til six tonight."

"Just come by my dorm room when you're finished with classes. My roommate and I plan to order-in pizza. Our room is two-twenty-four." Kara knew nothing about this impromptu plan. I devised it as a means of including Leah.

"Sure. Sounds good." She hiked her backpack on. "Thanks. I'll see you guys later."

We parted, each going in a different direction. Out of the corner of my eye, I watched Leah, noting her straight, almost stilted posture and long controlled strides, walking as if on guard. I gradually lost sight of her, buried in a multitude of students rushing to classes. I sensed she felt lost and alone among the crowd.

I texted Kara, briefly relaying that I extended a pizza invitation to Leah. Kara texted back: *Free for pizza tonight!*

Entering my classroom, I was deep in thought, having a hard time forgiving Nathan.

That evening, Kara returned from her last class shortly before six. I filled her in on my morning conversation with Leah. We decided to order the pizza because, even if Leah didn't show, we were starving.

After ordering, Kara and I prayed that the conversation with Leah would happen and bring God glory. Moments later, we heard a knock.

I opened the door to find Leah standing in the hall, biting her lower lip.

"Hey! Come in! Let me introduce you to my roommate, Kara Williamson. Kara, this is Leah Morris.

"Nice to meet you, Kara."

"Good to meet you, Leah." Kara pulled out her desk chair. "Take this chair. It's way more comfortable than Brooke's. We ordered pizza, which should be delivered soon."

Leah sat with a straight posture and clasped her hands on her lap.

We exchanged small talk about our classes. When I brought up my World Religion class and how the professor seemed to have a New Age worldview, Leah commented, "I've heard of New Age, but don't know much about it. What exactly is it?"

I pulled my hair behind my ear. "My understanding is it's made up of spiritual seekers who think that every part of existence connects to a single, divine whole. Divinity is found inside the person and can be reached through self-knowledge. These spiritual seekers believe that people are free to believe in whatever religious practice fits their lives." I stretched my legs and arms. "A friend of mine, one of these spiritual seekers, once told me that all paths, including Buddhism, Judaism, Hinduism, and Christianity, lead to that god. But in thinking so, they're essentially rejecting Christianity because Jesus said, 'I am the way, and the truth, and the life. No one comes to the Father except through me.'"

Leah leaned in. "Did you tell your friend that Jesus said that?"

"Yep, that's when she told me I was being closed-minded. I told her I was quoting Jesus, the very one she acknowledged was a prophet and great teacher. I don't know, the conversation went round and round."

"You know"—Leah placed her index finger on her lips—"that sounds like what my dad believes."

Kara was propped up on floor pillows, looking up at Leah. "What are your thoughts on it, Leah?"

"I haven't thought about it lately. My grandma loved to read the Bible and would share verses with me all the time. She was an amazing woman." Leah looked between Kara and me. "Are you Christians?"

Kara and I answered without hesitation, in unison. "Yes."

Kara's phone beeped with a text alert. She read it and stood up. "That's the pizza guy. He's out front. I'll be right back."

While we waited for Kara and the pizza, I asked, "Would you like to join us for church on Sunday?"

"Sure! I'd like that. Thanks. I know we've just met, but I feel like, I don't know, you remind me of my best friend from home, back when we were close. I haven't really connected with anyone here, at least not in a good way. My sorority sisters barely associate with me. When they do, it seems contrived, probably because I'm a legacy. To be honest, I've been thinking about dropping out of school, but I'm not sure how that would solve anything." Leah paused to clear her throat. "Maybe Christian friends, if they're like you and Kara, are what I need."

"I think you're right. We all need Christian friends to surround us. Is your best friend from home a Christian?"

"We used to talk about God, and her mom took us to church occasionally. But we've lost touch since she got pregnant then got married last year. We don't have much in common anymore. The couple of times I've called her, she seemed preoccupied with taking care of her baby." Leah glanced down and shuffled her feet on our shag rug. "I enrolled here to get away from my hometown. I haven't connected with my high school classmates in a while. Moving here was a way to make a fresh start." She shrugged. "It's not been a great start though."

My heart was breaking for Leah. This beautiful girl, who appeared to have it all, seemed so lonely.

I placed my palms on my knees and leaned forward. "I hope we can hang out more. The church service we attend starts at nine on Sunday mornings. My sorority big sis, Maddi, picks us up here at the dorm at quarter 'til nine. I'd love it if you could join us."

Leah's face lit up. "That'd be great."

Kara heard the last of our conversation as she returned with the pizza. The tiny dorm room exploded with the aromas of oregano and tomato sauce.

As we indulged in warm, gooey cheese and zesty pepperoni, I said, "I'm thinking it's the guilt of eating this pizza that's making me want to work out at the gym."

Kara and Leah tittered.

"No, really, y'all. I'm serious!"

Kara turned to Leah, "We work out at Gregory gym a couple of nights a week. Do you work out there?"

"No, I've just been going to the dorm workout room."

Kara picked up her Diet Coke. "Maybe you could join us the next time we go. The cute guys are definitely a perk in joining the gym."

Kara and I exchanged our cell numbers with Leah so we could text her when we planned to work out. After finishing off the pizza, we agreed that we probably should consider going soon.

10

I squinted through half-opened eyes, trying to adjust to the light of the sunshine relentlessly beaming through the window. The delicate, sheer curtains I'd insisted on buying for the dorm window provided little coverage. Chic but not especially functional. Gradually realizing it was Sunday morning and time to get ready for church, I rolled out of bed and headed for the bathroom. I was still trying to wake up as I smeared toothpaste on my toothbrush. Going through the brushing motions, my mind wandered to the previous week. It had been a good one.

Leah had joined Kara and me at the gym a couple of times.

I met Mark for lunch on Wednesday. He'd become a good friend, like the brother I never had.

Kara and Abbey partnered with me in searching Scripture to find Jesus's instructions on forgiveness. They prayed with me as I sought to fully forgive Nathan.

Thursday night, Kara and I caught a ride with Maddi to attend our community group. At the end of our study, we considered the assigned discussion questions: "How can we, as a group, serve our community? How can we show God's love by serving as a support to those in need?"

Abbey proposed that the group gather outside the local Planned Parenthood facility to offer young women comfort and prayer.

Everyone had liked the idea and agreed to meet at the church a week from Saturday.

Dressed and ready for church, Kara and I met Leah down in the lobby. We waited in front of the dorm for Maddi. Inhaling the crisp autumn air heightened my excitement that Leah was joining us for the church service.

We piled into the car and introduced Leah and Maddi. Leah seemed to be at ease as Maddi asked about where she was from and what she was studying.

I took in the fluttering orange and yellow leaves of the maple trees lining the road. The brilliant colors dazzled in the morning sun.

At the church, our friends greeted Leah and showed genuine interest in her. Her eyes sparkled, and her skin shone radiantly as she connected with them. Mark was among the friends gathered.

I'd noticed he'd been staring at her since she'd arrived. "Hey, I think we're in the same Spanish class."

"I knew that was you!" Leah grinned and added, lightheartedly, "*Como esta, Senor?*"

Mark laughed. "*Bien, gracias!* . . .Yep, that's the extent of my Spanish."

Their laughter added to the buzz of cheerful conversations in the church lobby. Mark and Leah continued to talk, leaning close together. Soft singing, drifting from the auditorium, was our cue that worship had begun. We slipped inside, found Abbey and John, and sat with them.

We were continuing the study series on Luke. The sermon, from chapter seven, was about a sinful woman forgiven by Jesus. At one point during the sermon, when Pastor David described the Pharisee who openly judged the woman, Leah lowered her head, eyes cast down on the opened Bible resting on her lap. She crossed her arms and sat rigid until Pastor David got to verse forty-eight where Jesus tells the woman, "Your sins are forgiven." Leah's posture relaxed.

After the sermon, we sang the hymn, "Come Thou Fount of Every

Blessing." I noticed Leah's eyes tearing when we got to the lyrics, "Bind my wandering heart to thee."

On the way home, Leah thanked us for inviting her. She seemed uplifted. "I loved going to church with you guys today!" She wrinkled her nose, and hesitated before asking, "Can I borrow a Bible from someone? My grandma gave me one, but I left it back home."

I handed her my Bible. "Please, Leah, take this one. I have another Bible in my room."

She smiled as she reached for it. "Thanks. I'll get it back to you tomorrow."

"No, Leah, it's yours to keep. I have the other one."

As we pulled up to the dorm, we all thanked Maddi for the ride.

"My pleasure! I'll be here to pick you all up next time. Hope you'll join us again, Leah."

"Thank you! I'd love to. It was nice meeting you."

Maddi smiled. "You too."

Once we were out of the car, Maddi rolled down the window. "Leah, there's a Bible class at the church starting in a couple of weeks on Monday evenings—seven o'clock. It's called Bible one-oh-one."

I adjusted my purse strap on my shoulder. "Yeah, it's basically a walk through the Bible. Kara and I just finished it. It was great!"

Maddi added, "I'd be happy to go through the class with you. Just let me know."

Leah froze, staring at Maddi. "Really? You would do that with me?"

"Of course, it'd be such a joy for me!"

Leah's eyes widened. "Thank you! That would be wonderful."

Genuine care radiated from Maddi's eyes. "I think so too."

Leah, Kara, and I went into the dorm and headed directly to the dining room. The delicious smells of roast beef and yeast rolls wafted through the hall.

Over lunch, Leah seemed excited. She posed questions about the sermon, so Kara and I opened the Bible and cross-referenced supporting scriptures. Leah leaned in, listening intently. She barely touched her food.

As we left the dining hall, I asked, "Do y'all want to work out at the gym sometime tomorrow?"

"I have a full day tomorrow," Leah said.

Kara shifted her Bible in her arms. "I'm out too. I'm meeting the guy from my biochemistry class at the library."

"Again?" Leah and I said in unison then broke into giggles.

"You two, stop!" Kara beamed a blushing smile.

We decided to go to the gym on Tuesday evening at five instead.

11

Tuesday evening, Kara and I sat in the lobby, waiting for Leah. It was after five, and she wasn't answering her phone. After waiting a while longer, I headed to her room.

As I approached her room, I heard sad music resonating through the door. I knocked, but she didn't answer. I called through the door, "Hey, Leah, you still coming to the gym with us?"

The music stopped, but only silence ensued. Finally, "No, I'm really tired. Just go without me, please."

She sounded different, like she'd been crying.

"Leah, are you okay?"

"I'm fine. I just don't feel like going tonight." I heard a catch in her voice, followed by sniffing.

I called a little louder, "Are you ill?" I couldn't keep the alarm out of my voice.

She cracked the door open, enough that I could see her tear-stained eyes and blotchy face. Worry filled me.

"I'm fine, really," she whispered.

"Is it Nathan? Did he upset you?"

She moaned. "I haven't seen him in almost two months. No, I . . . I just need to be alone."

I regretted bringing up Nathan. I didn't know what to say, so I spoke from my heart. "How can I pray for you?"

She opened the door a little more. "I don't know. I just . . . I guess I need to know God is here."

I prayed aloud, "Gracious God, thank You for being present, even when we don't feel Your presence. Psalm one forty-five verse eighteen tells us You are near to all who call on You in truth. Please, Lord, make Your presence known to Leah. As she seeks You, please give her the depth of comfort that only You, Father, can provide. I pray these things in the name of Your Son, Jesus. Amen."

Leah opened the door and hugged me. She seemed to hang on to me as if afraid to let go. But she eventually stepped back. "Thank you, Brooke. You have no idea what your friendship means to me. Look, I'll be fine. I just need to get some rest."

"Are you sure you don't want to talk about anything? I'm here if you need to."

"I know you are. I'll call you in the morning." She seemed to force a smile, then she slowly closed the door.

Sadness overcame me. It was gut-wrenching.

I slowly walked away, texting Kara. *"Going to our room to pray."*

I received Kara's reply. *"Meet you there."*

12

The next day, I was completely zoned out. I watched my professor's lips moving but didn't process anything he said. All I could do was think about how upset Leah was the night before. I wished I knew what was going on with her. I took comfort in knowing that God did.

It was already two-thirty, and Leah hadn't called as promised. She had classes, but if I hadn't heard from her by three, I planned to call her.

Class released at quarter to three, and as I left the classroom, my phone beeped. It was her.

"Leah!"

"Hey, Brooke. I apologize for my crazy emotions last night. I guess I was just tired. Anyway, thank you for stopping by and praying. It meant a lot."

She didn't sound like herself. Her voice was high pitched, and she sounded out of breath. Maybe she was walking between classes.

"I'm so glad you called. Are you feeling better?"

"Yeah, it's amazing what a good night's sleep will do. Hey, I'm getting ready to walk into my next class. I'll see you later."

"Yeah, take care." Something wasn't right. I felt it in my core.

It was a short five-minute walk back to the dorm. Approaching the dorm entrance, I glanced up to the second story windows. I stopped abruptly when I caught sight of Leah pacing back and forth at her dorm window, her phone to her ear. *What is going on, Leah? You just lied to me!*

Turning in her pace, she glanced out the window. Our eyes locked. She stood still. She slowly lowered her phone and her free hand shot to her mouth.

I jerked my head sideways, averting my eyes. I blew through my nostrils then bolted into the dorm. I took the stairwell, two steps at a time, up to my room. I locked my door then went limp, knees to the floor. *No matter if she texts, calls or even knocks on the door, I'm not answering.*

Didn't matter. None of those happened. Hurt didn't come close to describing my feelings. I was done with her.

13

Seven forty-five on Saturday morning rolled around way too early, especially after attending another mixer until late the night before.

My community group members were arriving at the church for the outreach and prayer vigil we'd scheduled at the Planned Parenthood facility. Two of the cars had babies safely buckled in their car seats because the couples couldn't find sitters. The Planned Parenthood staff permitted us to park our cars on the outlying perimeter, off of the facility's property.

When our caravan arrived, a dozen cars were already in the parking lot. I wondered how many of those belonged to staff and how many had transported mothers and their unborn babies. We parked off of the property and set up lawn chairs and card tables, putting out orange juice and bagels. We paired off and began to pray for God's protection for the unborn babies and comfort for the women in need.

By ten o'clock, two young women had come over to talk. The Pates were praying with one of the women. Maddi and Abbey had been talking with the other woman for at least thirty minutes, sharing Scripture and praying. Once they finished praying, Maddi and Abbey hugged the woman. She smiled through tears, nodding her head. She headed toward her car but stopped to smile at one of our couple's baby, who cooed in his stroller. As she admired the baby boy, she dropped her head and cried. Abbey reached out to embrace her again.

I looked past Abbey to see a taxi pulling up to the building. A woman emerged from the back seat on the far side of the car. I couldn't see her face. As she climbed the front steps of the building, the taxi driver pulled out of the parking lot. The tall, slender woman never turned around. She pulled open the front door and rushed inside.

"I gotta go," I said to Kara over my shoulder as I dashed across the parking lot. I swung open the door, but the woman was nowhere in sight.

I stopped at the information desk. "Which direction to the abortion clinic?"

The receptionist crossed her arms over her ample chest. "Do you have an appointment?"

My mind raced. "I'm here for my friend. She was just dropped off."

She pursed her lips then waved her hand as if shooing a fly. "Two doors down the hall to your right."

I followed her directions and quietly stepped into the waiting room. Several women sat waiting in plush upholstered armchairs.

I gasped as I saw Leah look up. We stared at each other.

I quickly crossed the room and sat beside her. I grabbed her hand and whispered, "Leah?"

Leah peered at me, then at the other women around the room, then back at me. Tears streamed down her face. She whispered, "You're here! I was too ashamed to tell you, Brooke. I regret everything. I just want this to go away." She stole a quick glance at the other women in the room and cupped her mouth with her palm, making her voice barely audible. "I'm torn. I don't know what else to do."

I couldn't find my breath. *Help, Lord!*

A sudden boldness came over me. "Come with me." I grabbed her hand and led her out of the waiting room to a secluded hallway bench.

She slumped on the bench next to me, covering her face with a wad of tissue.

I placed my hand on her back and whispered, "Leah, talk to me, please!"

Her eyes found mine. Those usually brilliant eyes were dulled with fear and sorrow. She spoke through the tears. "I'm pregnant. I suspected it when I missed my period twice, but on Monday the doctor confirmed it. The father is Nathan."

Her breathing accelerated and deepened, as if she couldn't get enough oxygen. "I called him Monday afternoon to see if he could meet me. He said he was too busy. So I told him over the phone." Tears spilled down her pale cheeks. "The very moment I said the word *pregnant*, he hung up. He didn't say a word. He just hung up on me."

I embraced Leah, letting her quietly sob on my shoulder. My breathing tightened and my heart pounded. I wanted to bolt out of there and hunt Nathan down. Then the Luke verse that had convicted me weeks before played over and over in my mind. *"Judge not, and you will not be judged. Judge not, and you will not be judged. . ."* Thank you, God, for your patience with me.

I tried to remember what Maddi had told me the night I danced with Nathan. What did she say? Something like, God knows and has a plan for me.

"Leah, God loves you. He has a plan for you and your baby. I promise to help you get the support you need. Can you go back to the dorm with me so we can pray and figure out what to do next?"

She stared at me, studied me, then slowly nodded her head. As if in a trance, she echoed my word. "Baby . . . my baby."

She tipped her head. She had a puzzled look. "How did you know I was here?"

"I didn't. I came with my community group this morning to offer support to women who might be contemplating abortion. I had no idea you'd be here until I thought I saw you getting out of a taxi."

Wrinkles formed on her forehead. "Do you mean all those people from church are outside?" Her face lost all color. "I can't go out there!"

"They are on the outskirts of the property. You don't have to face them. Do you want me to call a taxi or text Maddi to pick us up?"

Leah buried her face in her hands, fresh tears flowed. She sagged, as if the burden she carried was far too heavy for her delicate frame. I rested my hand on her shoulder and silently prayed, *Heavenly Father, I ask that You provide Leah with strength, wisdom, and discernment for her and her baby's good, but, most importantly, for Your glory. Please have her experience Your love now. Please make Your presence known to her. Have her make the right choice of keeping her baby and, as she makes that choice, bring her a comfort and peace that only You can provide. We need You, Lord.*

Leah remained still. Staring at the ball of tissue clenched in her hands, she whispered, "This is only the beginning of my shame." She shook her head and squeezed her eyes shut. "Let's just call a cab."

I called for the taxi then texted Kara: *With a friend—needs discretion—watch for taxi then gather group in prayer.*

Kara acknowledged. *K—will do.*

Once Leah and I stepped out front, we slipped into the taxi. I looked back. The group had gathered in a circle, heads bowed in prayer.

Once we made it to Leah's room, she collapsed on her bed and stared into space. Her limp body was motionless, and her swollen eyes seemed to have no more tears. In a raspy voice, she whispered, "I don't know how I'm going to do this. I'm so scared. My parents will stop paying for my schooling when they find out."

I knelt by Leah's bed and prayed aloud. "Dear Lord, please provide Leah with Your comfort, peace, and provision. Please provide us with discernment and direct us to sources of assistance. Thank You for creating us according to Your perfect will and plan and loving us unconditionally. Thank You for being our sovereign God, always in control. Thank You for being present and making a way for us through Your Son, Jesus."

Leah rested her hands over her eyes, remaining still and quiet.

I searched the internet on her laptop, typing in *help for unwed pregnancy*. An array of resources popped up.

I turned the screen so Leah could see the long list of services available: financial planning assistance, free counseling, free medical-prenatal care, college financing, affordable baby and children's clothing and supplies, job search assistance, and even information on Christian adoption agencies.

Leah uncovered her eyes and looked over my shoulder as I scrolled through the information. She didn't say a word. Then she moaned and fell back onto the bed.

I'd pushed her too far, offering too much too soon. Why did I bombard her? She just needed time to process the news without figuring out the next step. I was so ill-equipped to help her.

Leah pulled herself up to sit on the side of her bed. She kept her head down, her gaze fixed on the floor. "I can't do this. I'm struggling . . . and there's nothing you can do to help me with that right now. I'm angry with God and a lot of people in my life." Without looking at me, she added, "It's not you though. Please know that. I just need time . . . time alone."

I closed the laptop. "All right." I hesitated to say the next thing, afraid to leave her alone. "I'll leave, but . . ."

"I promise not to do anything rash. I know I haven't been honest with you lately, but I'm promising now." Her voice was monotone, void of emotion.

I looked down at my white knuckles and realized I was gripping the laptop. I placed it on her desk. "I'll be praying."

She finally gave me eye contact. "I know. I need time. Then I'll call you." Her face was ashen.

I reached for her hand but only our fingertips touched before she coiled her hands under her knees. She gazed back at the floor.

I slowly shuffled out of the room, willing my legs to move. *Dear God, help her.*

14

I was alone in my room Sunday afternoon after having slept only an hour or two the night before. My sadness over Leah's situation was followed by a yearning to do something to help, and a feeling of despair in knowing that I couldn't.

Somehow, I had managed to go to church with Kara that morning, knowing I couldn't share my grief with anyone. Leah's news needed to remain confidential.

After Kara left for the library, I kneeled to pray for Leah and her unborn child. The words didn't come easy—the tears did.

I tried to concentrate on school assignments. For my World Religion class, the assignment was to document supporting evidence for the statement: "There is no one true way to achieve spiritual fulfillment." The more Bible verses came to mind, the faster my fingers typed and the angrier I became. I didn't care if I received a failing grade. It would be my first, but it would be worth it. This professor was going to read what the Bible had to say about his messed-up assignment.

Lord, how can this professor be allowed to mislead hundreds, even thousands of students? How can Nathan be allowed to deceive so many women? Lord, where are You in all of this?

I closed my laptop and stared out the window into darkness. How did I miss the sunset? Silence permeated the room, yet noise filled my head. I couldn't even pray anymore.

Pacing between the door and the window—my motions were aimless. My imagination was wreaking havoc with my mind. Was Leah all right? She promised she wouldn't do anything rash, but she'd lied to me before.

I grabbed my phone and scrolled to search for Nathan's number. *It's time you hear from me, you cruel liar!*

Then I heard a soft knock. I put my phone down. I rushed to the door and flung it open. Leah stood in the hall, hands clenching the Bible I had given her. It was pressed against her chest. I grasped her shoulders and guided her into my room.

She stood motionless in the middle of the room; shoulders slumped. "Brooke, when you prayed yesterday, thanking God for being sovereign and present, I was reminded of a passage my grandma used to recite." She opened the Bible to a bookmarked page: Psalm 139:11-14. "'If I say, 'surely the darkness shall cover me, and the light about me be night,' even the darkness is not dark to You; the night is bright as the day, for darkness is as light with You. For You formed my inward parts; You knitted me together in my mother's womb. I praise You, for I am fearfully and wonderfully made. Wonderful are Your works; my soul knows it very well.' Brooke, when Grandma would recite those verses, I thought it was all about me. 'God made you wonderfully,' Grandma would say over and over. But those verses are about how God is in control. He created my baby. He's been present with my baby in the darkness of my womb before I even knew I was pregnant." Leah's wide eyes fixed on mine. "I can't abort this baby."

I'm certain my face showed my shock in God's answer to my prayers. *Thank You, God, for Your Word and for Leah's grandma!* Tears filled my eyes.

Leah hugged me. "Thank you, Brooke, for showing up yesterday. You saved me from making a horrible choice. You . . . you saved my baby's life."

I shook my head. "No, God saved your baby's life. Seriously, it was solely by His grace. I was really botching things up, but God turned it around for your good and the good of your unborn child."

Leah closed her eyes, and, for the first time, I heard her pray aloud,

"Thank You, God, for placing Brooke in my life. Thank You, God, for protecting my baby. I . . . I'm overwhelmed by Your presence. Thank You for being a good Father. Please stay close to me, God."

We opened the Bible and read more from the book of Psalms. What an amazing time we had giving glory to God.

PART II

Leah

15

November 2004
Austin, Texas

The heartbeat was strong and rapid, like an underwater gallop. Hearing it for the first time convinced me to keep my baby rather than pursue adoption. My doctor calculated the due date to be the first of June.

One of the hardest things I had to do was tell my parents. I felt suspended in an eerie calm before the inevitable storm. I wished I could just stay in the calm, but the only way through the storm was through it.

I flew home to New York the first weekend in November. Sitting in the shadows of our breakfast room, a rush of childhood memories flooded me, as if a dam had burst. I recalled times when things seemed brighter and less complicated. I remembered my childhood excitement of scattering red sprinkles on heart-shaped cookies, blowing out birthday candles, and running down the hall in anticipation of what Santa had left under the tree. I grieved the loss of those early carefree years.

Mom set two cans of soda and a tray of fruit on the table. She then eased into the chair beside me. She seemed to move slower than when

I last saw her, just three months ago. Her midsection bulged slightly as she slumped in the chair.

"You must be hungry and exhausted after your long flight. Please, honey, eat something."

"Thanks, Mom." I bit into an apple slice.

Mom took a sip of her soda and tapped her house shoes on the worn area rug. She dabbed her mouth with a napkin, then folded it on her lap. As she tilted her chin down, I could see gray roots at the crown of her head. She looked up at me, shifting forward, not blinking . . . waiting.

My coming home at the beginning of November was not in the budget. Holiday trips home, yes. Weekend trips, no. She knew something was up.

"Mom, I need you now and I hope you'll forgive me. I made a huge misjudgment, trusting in a man I shouldn't have. It resulted in my wrong decision to continue drinking a drink he'd fixed for me. Because of that decision, I'm pregnant."

After an agonizing pause, she whispered hoarsely, "Oh, Leah." She leaned back into her chair as if struck by an invisible hand. "What have you done? How could you?"

I looked down at my fidgeting fingers and the ring that Grandma had given me shined in the sunlight that flickered through the window. "I wasn't wise to trust the guy. After several sips of the drink, the room started spinning. I don't remember anything after that. He didn't want to have anything to do with me the next day."

"Who is this man? He sounds like a rapist. Has he tried to contact you?"

"No. I called him to tell him I'm pregnant and he hung up on me."

"Oh, no! Don't call him again. I'm not sure you should even return to school."

"Why should I quit school? What would that solve? I need to pursue a career to support this child."

Mom stared at me like I was some sort of circus freak. Then she crossed her arms and leaned forward. "There are adoption agencies—"

"No. I've thought long and hard about this. . .I've prayed about this. I'm keeping this child, and I'm going to raise this child."

Her gaze slowly swept downward, as if trying to find a misplaced puzzle piece on the floor. I knew seconds, even minutes, were passing as I heard the rhythmic ticking of the grandfather clock in the foyer. Finally, she spoke. "Are . . . are you healthy? Is the baby all right?"

"We're both fine. I just need you now, Mom, . . . your support, your love."

Seeming to come to some conclusion, she straightened and rested her eyes on me. It was the same gentle look she gave me when I had come home from school crying because Claire, my best friend from kindergarten, had told me that she was moving away, and we couldn't be friends anymore.

She lunged forward in her chair and embraced me. "Leah, I'm here for you."

"Thank you." I had forgotten her embrace. It now seemed unfamiliar, yet welcomed. "Thank you, Mom."

When I called Dad, however, he made it clear he wasn't going to provide any more financial support. "After all, I have young children now and you're an adult, Leah. You got yourself into this. You need to figure out how to take care of yourself and that kid."

It pained me that he referred to his grandchild as "that kid."

"Believe me, Dad, I will. I'll let you go. Goodbye."

Mom, sitting next to me, overheard his harsh remarks. She put her arm around my shoulder. "I'll pay for your tuition. I won't be able to pay for the sorority or dorm fees though."

"Thank you. I don't care about the sorority. I've not connected with any of my sorority sisters anyway. Dorm fees for Hardin House are paid up through the end of spring semester, so I can live in the dorm until then. I'll get a part-time job to cover my cost of living expenses and help with the tuition."

Mom dropped her arm from my shoulder and rubbed the back of her neck. Her drooping eyelids made her look old and exhausted.

Experiencing my father's rejection once again, this time as his daughter with child, I finally was able to empathize with Mom. It struck me how deep Mom's grief must have been when my father ran off with another woman and left her with a child to raise on her own. As a girl, when I turned to Mom for comfort, she was essentially unavailable. She was probably emotionally drained and overwhelmed at suddenly being a single parent. As I reflected, I realized that my dad had abandoned both of us, but Mom had the added burden of single parenthood. Of all the people in my life, she understood best what I was facing.

More than the financial and emotional support I received from Mom was the healing that took place in my heart for her. How could I have been so unforgiving toward her? I guess I'd been sorely immature.

Sunday morning, Mom and I attended church together, something we hadn't done since I was a child.

When it was time for me to board the plane departing for Austin, we hugged each other and softly wept. A tight bond had formed between us. Mother and daughter for sure, but also woman to woman.

"I love you, Leah. I hope I'll be a better grandmother than I've been a mother."

"I love you too, Mom. I love that you're my mom."

16

When I returned to Austin, things started looking up.

Brooke, using Abbey's car, drove me to my doctor's appointments and prayed with me countless times.

The first Monday night back, I attended the Bible class with Maddi.

Brooke's friend, Mark, also attended. After the first week, he offered me rides to class, and we hung out afterwards. I enjoyed time with Mark. He had a fun personality and a contagious smile. His kind blue eyes and shallow-arched brows softened his angular jawline.

Sharing yogurt with him after class one night, I couldn't contain my excitement about the lesson. "Mark, the Bible patriarchs and their families were so flawed. I never knew Abraham, Isaac, and Jacob had such crazy sin in their lives."

"I know. The stories of the people in the Bible continue to give me assurance that God is able to redeem even me of my sin."

"What do you mean? You're the perfect church guy. I don't know why you're in this beginner's Bible class."

"Well, first, I'm not the perfect church guy. I'm a sinner in need of a savior and Bible study points me to my savior, Jesus. Second, I'll never know all there is to know about the Bible and attending a class keeps me accountable to study it regularly. And third, I'm new to this church congregation so this class has been a great way for me to get to know the people who attend, especially you." Mark smiled with a sparkle in his eyes.

He took a bite of his yogurt, dripping some on his shirt. ". . .and I'm a slob." He grabbed a napkin and dabbed the spot. Then he grabbed another napkin and covered his face, pretending to be embarrassed. My laughter spilled out, as if it had been bottled up too long.

As Mark and I met several times each week, and we discussed our class assignments, I became amazed at his insight into the Scriptures. I checked with Brooke to make sure they were just friends before I continued accepting his calls. Our relationship was growing into more than just a friendship.

I was baptized the third Sunday of November. Mark seemed overwhelmed with happiness. What a day!

I also started going to community group at Michael and Caroline Pate's home with Kara, Brooke, and Maddi. Mark planned to join us in December, after his Thursday night men's Bible study was over.

I found it extremely difficult to admit my pregnancy to my community group. But since everyone was transparent in sharing personal stories of brokenness, I finally shared mine.

We were all in awe of God's perfect timing and provision because the night I told the group of my pregnancy, Michael and Caroline offered me a part-time babysitting position to care for their two children, Becca, age four, and Zeke, age two. Their babysitter had recently submitted her resignation due to health issues. The Pates had interviewed intensively to fill the position but hadn't found a suitable candidate, one whom they felt they could trust.

The Pates took me aside. "We've seen how wonderfully you've interacted with our children. Of course, we want to give you time to pray before deciding," Michael said.

"But I must tell you," Caroline added, "Michael and I have been praying, especially after the last discouraging interview, that God would send us someone who seeks Him and His Word. The position would include maternity leave and, once you return to school, you and I could switch off who watches our two little ones and your baby. Since I work part-time and my schedule is flexible, I could watch all three while you're in class."

Caroline and Michael even offered me their garage apartment as part of my compensation.

After praying about the offer, I accepted the position the next morning. Since freshmen were required to live on campus and my housing at Hardin House was paid up through May, I planned to move into the Pates' garage apartment at the end of May. That would allow me time to get settled before the baby arrived in June. With the arrangement, I'd be able to continue with school.

God was being faithful to provide for my needs. But my faith still wavered. I was uncertain how all of this would end up.

17

"Happy Thanksgiving, Leah!" Caroline said on the phone. "I have two very excited little ones here wanting to talk to you."

"Aw, Caroline, put them on!"

"Happy Fanksgiving, Miss Leah!" came Becca's soft little voice.

In the background, I heard Zeke's shouts. "Weyah! Weyah!"

Becca reprimanded her little brother. "Zeke, not Weyah! It's Leah!"

I snickered. "Happy Thanksgiving, Becca and Zeke!"

They were the cutest, with their giggles and bouncing joy.

Caroline's voice came back on the phone. "I know Mark will be picking you up soon, so we'll let you go. Hope you enjoy the day!"

"Oh, Caroline! That was so sweet! I just saw Becca and Zeke yesterday, but I already miss them. Thanks for calling and have a blessed day!"

I was loving my new babysitting position.

I couldn't afford to fly home for the holiday since I had gone several weeks before. When Mark learned that I'd be alone, he asked me to join him and his family for Thanksgiving dinner. I went down to the lobby to wait for him.

Exiting the elevator, I spotted Mark entering the lobby. I stopped in my tracks, taken in, again, by his striking good looks.

"Happy Thanksgiving!" Mark gave me an affectionate hug, and then we were on our way.

The Taylors lived in a beautiful home in the hills of Austin. His dad had designed the house. Admiring the multi-level layout, it was easy to see why Mr. Taylor was such a successful architect. An additional amenity was the view from the back patio of the UT tower. Breath-taking.

The Taylors showed me such kindness. Mark's younger sister, Hannah, was a junior in high school and full of energy. Mrs. Taylor, the sweetest lady, so gracious and hospitable, made me feel immediately at home. It was remarkable how much Mark was like his dad, a perfect gentleman.

Before dinner, Mr. Taylor led us in a beautiful prayer of thanksgiving. After closing with "Amen," he said, "Let's dig in!"

The dinner was amazing! For dessert, I brought pecan spice cookies that I had baked in the Pate's kitchen the day before. Mrs. Taylor had prepared a yummy pumpkin pie.

"Leah, I would love the recipe for your cookies. They're delicious!" Mrs. Taylor said, reaching for a second one.

"You're very kind, Mrs. Taylor. But, seriously, my half-burned cookies couldn't hold a candle to your pumpkin pie! It's the best ever!"

Mr. Taylor furrowed his brows. "Burned? I scarfed down five of those cookies!" He held up his empty plate. "Aw, I must have not liked them." His hearty laughter was contagious.

And we all laughed and talked, fully engaged, into the evening.

As Mark drove me back to campus, I said, "Your mom and sister were talking about your family's church. It sounds amazing with all its ministries and outreach programs!"

"It is. After attending that church all my life, I struggled to connect with a church near campus. I visited several but didn't feel welcomed. I don't know, maybe it was my critical attitude. But when I visited our campus church, I was welcomed right away."

"That's exactly how I felt about our campus church, but then, I didn't have another church to compare it to. I was so young when my family attended church together. I don't remember much about it."

Mark pulled up to my dorm.

"Mark, I had so much fun today. Your family is great!"

"I could tell they liked you a lot." Mark turned off the ignition then shifted in his seat to face me. He looked at me timidly. "Would you be my date to the Garth Brooks concert? It's on December eleventh."

Unbelievable! Not only were we parked in the same driveway that Nathan had rudely peeled out of the last morning I was with him, but this was the same concert Nathan promised he would take me to.

"I would love to go with you. Is it okay if I let you know tomorrow after I check my babysitting schedule?"

"Absolutely." A deep smile spread over Mark's face.

He got out and, as he walked around the car to open my door, my mind raced. The babysitting thing was just an excuse. I was 99 percent sure I wouldn't be babysitting that Saturday. If I was going to be honest with Mark, I'd have to tell him of my pregnancy. I wasn't sure how.

He opened my car door and walked me to the dorm's porch, where he wrapped me in a warm embrace. I felt safe in his strong arms.

"I'll call you tomorrow. Goodnight, Leah."

This guy was the kindest man I'd ever known. "Thank you again for a wonderful Thanksgiving. I enjoyed being with you and your family today." I pulled away. "Goodnight, Mark."

I walked through the lobby, feeling unsettled. Our relationship was becoming more than just a casual friendship. He deserved to know. How could I tell him? How would he take it? What would he think of me?

Once I reached my room, I called Brooke. In giddy Brooke fashion, she answered, "Happy Thanksgiving, girl! What's up?"

"Hey, I just realized I may be interrupting your Thanksgiving dinner." I scrunched my nose and hoped I wasn't.

"Oh, no. We finished hours ago. Right now, we're just watching nonstop football and looking like stuffed zombies. How are you?"

"I'm good! I had the most amazing day with Mark and his family. But he just asked me out to the Garth Brooks concert."

"Leah, that's great! But I don't get it. Why do you sound concerned?"

"I don't know how to answer Mark. He still doesn't know I'm pregnant. If I turn him down, he'll think I don't care about him, and I sure don't want that. If I accept his invitation, I'll have to tell him I'm pregnant first. It's only right. I'm going to have to tell him eventually. I just don't think I'm ready to tell him yet. What should I do?"

"I think you should be upfront with him, Leah. You just said it. You're gunna have to tell him sooner or later. I think it would be better sooner rather than later. When you and Mark are together at church, I can see he cares for you, and not just as a friend. You don't want to tell him after he joins our community group, and you sure don't want to tell him after you start to show, right?"

"You're right. You're right." I placed my palm on my ribs, inhaled and puffed out a sigh. "You sound like my sage, always on point, grandma. If she were here, she'd quote a Sir Walter . . . somebody; 'Oh, what a tangled web we weave, when first we practice to deceive.'"

"I wish I could have met your grandma!"

18

The next day, I was still struggling with how I would tell Mark. I had spent the night rehearsing different ways, and none sounded good. How could they? This was a huge mess. I realized the moment I shared the news with him, our relationship would likely be over.

My phone rang and I saw his name on the caller ID. Here goes.

"Hi, Mark."

"Hey! How's your day going?"

"Fine. I'm still thinking about that delicious meal your mom prepared yesterday."

"It was great being with you. Did you have a chance to check your babysitting schedule?"

"Um, yeah." *Stop stalling!* "Well, I was wondering if we could meet somewhere to talk."

"Uh, sure . . . everything okay?"

"I just need to talk with you about something and it'd be better if I told you in person."

There was silence on his end that seemed to last an eternity.

"Mark?"

"Yeah, sure. How about we meet at the gazebo on Town Lake . . . about an hour?"

"Yes, that'll work. Thank you."

"All right. See you at four."

After we hung up, I stared at the wall. A sense of foreboding swept over me. Our relationship was about to end.

At a quarter 'til four, I found Mark leaning against one of the stone pillars that supported the gazebo. His arms were crossed, accentuating his broad shoulders and defined muscles evident through his T-shirt.

I walked toward him and smiled. "Hi."

He returned a half-smile. "Hi." Creases had formed on his forehead. "What . . . what's up?"

I felt my lower lip stinging and realized I was biting it. "Do you mind if we sit?"

Mark led me to a bench in the gazebo, all the while looking down.

I hated that I'd caused him such uneasiness. He sat next to me, his palms pressing his thighs, as if readying to get up and hurry away.

I swallowed hard, took a deep breath, and plunged into my rehearsed opening. "This is hard. What I'm about to tell you will likely change our relationship." *Breathe. Breathe!* "Before I met you, I allowed myself to get into a bad situation. I was dating a guy, a senior here on campus, and, well, one night I accepted a soda from him. Shortly after taking several sips, I began to feel strange. I should have known to throw away the soda because the more I drank, the more disoriented I became. The next thing I knew, it was morning, and I was in the guy's bed."

Mark's eyes widened.

I spoke hurriedly. "I'm pregnant with that man's baby."

Stillness hung on, as if time had stopped.

Mark finally exhaled like he'd been kicked in the gut. His jaw clenched and unclenched. He stood and walked to the edge of the gazebo, leaning into his forearm draped high on the pillar.

Then he walked down the gazebo steps and kept walking across the lawn.

Like every other man I'd ever cared about, he was leaving.

He turned back abruptly; his piercing blue eyes held mine. "It was date rape."

I slowly nodded, pressing my lips tightly together.

He ran his hands through his hair. "Have you reported this to the police?"

"No, I . . . I haven't. I won't. I'm partly to blame. I misjudged the man's motives. Or maybe I was hoping for a commitment that just wasn't there." I looked down at my feet and shuffled them. "I was the one who kept drinking the soda."

Striding back to the gazebo, he said, "Leah, he was the one who spiked the drink without your knowing, caused you to become disoriented, poisoned and raped you." He stopped at the steps.

"I'm not going to the police. I need to get on with my life. I need to take care of my baby." I looked up at him. My tears spilled over. I tasted the saltiness.

"You're keeping the baby?" His voice had softened.

I nodded rapidly. Our eyes remained fixed as he crossed the deck and sat down beside me.

Blinking, he drew me close into an affectionate hug and I could hear his labored breathing. Then I felt his lips on my forehead . . . *What? I so didn't deserve this kindness.* My emotions reeled. Remorse, sorrow, distress. I looked down at my hands clasped on my lap, the sight of them blurred through the tears I couldn't stop.

He released me. "The man you're talking about, is he still in the picture?"

I somehow found my voice, "No, I never heard from him after that morning when he dropped me at my dorm and sped off. I met you after that." I heaved a shaky sigh. "Then later, I found out I was pregnant. I called him, thinking he should know. But he hung up on me."

Mark embraced me again. I felt his heart pounding. He remained silent for a long time. Of course, he needed time to process it all. And he was probably trying to figure out how to say goodbye.

Finally, he sat back and looked me square in the eyes. "I promise, I'll stay by your side through this."

My hand reflexively covered my heart. I searched his eyes, seeing only genuine compassion. I slowly scrunched my face. "Well, not through the actual birth. We don't know each other that well."

Mark gave a slight smile. "I know." He gently swept my hair away from my cheek. "I'll be with you for as much as you want me to be. And God will remain with you."

"Thank you." I released my hand from across my chest. "God will remain with me. . .that reminds me of a Bible verse Brooke shared a while back. 'The Lord is near to all who call on Him . . .'" I squinted. "What's the rest?"

Mark held my hand. "'. . .To all who call on Him in truth.' Psalm one forty-five verse eighteen. It's one of my favorites. We'll keep calling on God in truth through Jesus Christ."

This man who usually seemed so upbeat now looked serious and seemed burdened. "Will you pray with me?"

I nodded.

He prayed an earnest prayer, asking God for His protection over me and the baby. When he closed, we sat in silence, admiring the silhouettes of birds that flew toward clouds tinged in various shades of magenta. Only the faint trill of the birds broke the stillness as the magnificent rays of the setting sun merged with the lake. Then looking out over the calm lake, we reflected on Scripture, long after the brilliance of the sun had set.

As night approached, Mark walked me back to my dorm, asking about my school plans. I told him about Mom's support, my new babysitting job, and plans of moving to the Pate's garage apartment. We talked about so many things, about the support of the community group and Brooke's relentless help in finding resources for me and the baby.

When we reached the dorm steps, Mark hugged me. "It sounds like things are working out, Leah. God is so good!"

I admired his kindness that beamed through his gentle eyes and genuine smile.

"Thank you for listening and praying for me and the baby."

"Thank you for sharing it all with me. Take care and let me know how I can help."

"I appreciate that, Mark."

"Goodbye."

In the lobby, I looked out the window and watched him walk away. His words echoed in my mind. *Take care. Goodbye.* No mention of plans for the next time we'd see each other. Things had changed and I sensed our relationship no longer held promise. When I reached my room, I called Brooke. She picked up on the first ring. "Hey! How'd it go?"

"It went fine. . .I guess. He seemed to be happy that I'm keeping the baby and he was, as usual, kind and caring. Yet, I don't know. . .especially toward the end, he acted distant. I was hoping for more than just a casual friendship."

"Did y'all talk about the concert?"

"No, he didn't bring it up again. I guess the date is off. This is hard. I care deeply for him."

"Maybe you're reading too much into it. Maybe he just forgot about the concert. Do you want me to call him?"

"No! Brooke! You have to promise me you won't."

"I promise. I won't. I don't break promises."

"I know you don't."

"I'll be praying."

"Thanks, Brooke. Talk to you later."

It was the worst tossing-and-turning night I'd experienced since the night of my grandma's funeral.

The next morning, I threw on some sweats and headed to the lobby. I needed coffee.

When the elevator doors opened, I froze. There stood Mark in the middle of the lobby. Joy and surprise washed over me, leaving me stunned. He held flowers wrapped in clear plastic and looked like a little boy presenting them to his first-grade teacher.

He spoke in a hoarse voice. "Hi. I—"

The elevator doors shut, and I was still standing like a statue in the elevator. *Oh, no!* Had I been standing there staring at Mark that long? I punched the lobby button. *Open! OPEN!* The doors finally eased open. "Mark!"

He dropped the flowers and grabbed me by my shoulders to pull me out. He picked up the flowers and handed them to me. Then he hugged me, crushing the flowers between us.

He leaned away then asked, "Will you be able to go to the concert with me?"

I couldn't find my breath. I was astonished. "You still want to take me after what I told you last night?"

"I've been anguishing over this all night. I regret that I didn't bring up the concert last night. Your news. . .well, it overwhelmed me."

"I understand." I looked down at my sweatshirt, tugging at the hem. "You don't have to—"

"I've never been more certain about wanting to take a woman on a date. I don't think anything could change that. Leah, will you be my date?"

Awed, I nodded excitedly. "I would love to go to the concert with you!"

He pulled me into a warm, comforting hug. He whispered, "Sorry I haven't showered. I've been up all night and stalking your dorm since dawn."

I snickered then covered my mouth. "I'm sorry too. I have morning breath."

I wished I could have stayed in that moment forever.

19

"If you keep moving, I'm liable to burn your face off with this curling iron."

"I'm just so excited! Mark will be picking me up for the concert in less than an hour!" I blurted to Brooke in an explosion of words, fidgeting in my seat.

"I know, Leah! That's why you need to hold still. We need to get you ready."

Brooke was helping me with my hair and makeup. The previous weekend, we had gone on a much-needed shopping trip since my clothes were beginning to fit too snugly. She had helped me assemble a cute outfit for the concert.

I was entering my second trimester, evidenced by a baby bump. The fact that it was my healthy, growing baby made it all good.

The money I'd earned from my job fully paid for all my purchases. Caroline and Michael were extremely generous in their compensation and accommodating in helping me coordinate my work and school schedules. With finals approaching, that was huge!

The Pates had also welcomed Mark into our community group. After group meeting one night, Brooke shared with Mark her bad experience with Nathan. Then Mark led Brooke and me in prayer to forgive Nathan.

Mark continued to stand by me, even as my pregnancy became

obvious. We had kissed only a couple of times, yet I loved him. We hadn't said those words to each other, but I sensed he felt the same.

Mark emulated what the Bible said a man of God should be. He honored me as Jesus honors the Church. God placed him in my life at a time when things seemed hopeless.

Thinking of these things, my lips trembled.

Brooke, looking at my reflection in the mirror, stopped fixing my hair. "Leah, what's wrong? You look like you're about to cry."

"I'm just so overwhelmed by God's blessings in my life. Quick, say something weird or funny so I won't cry and mess up the makeup you just applied!"

"Hold on." She grabbed my liquid eyeliner and painted a curly mustache above her lip. "Do you think my date will notice I have a mustache?"

That did the trick. We both burst out laughing.

"Oh, Brooke! Now we're going to have to fix your makeup! How can you be up on the latest hair and makeup trends yet have a roommate who dons a baseball cap and is ready to go?"

"Yep, we've been friends since junior high but we're polar opposites. I finally found out the last name of Kara's biochemistry class boyfriend. It's Lott. Michael Lott. I've been teasing Kara that her name would one day be Dr. Kara Lott. With that name, she'll have a booming medical practice."

"Ha! That's funny! Are you excited about going to the concert with Michael's friend, Drew?"

"Yeah, he's a nice guy." Brooke cupped her hand over my eyes and misted my hair with hairspray.

"I doubt Mark and I will get to see the four of you since the Frank Erwin Center is huge."

Lord, thank You for placing these Christian friends in my life. I realize it's all You, but they were responsive to the instructions of Your Word, to be kind to someone in need.

When Mark called to say he'd arrived, I flew down to the lobby.

He kissed my cheek. "You look beautiful." He led me by the hand out the door.

A stirring fluttered inside me. *Was that my excitement or could that have been the baby moving?* Mark opened the car door and helped me in. We were on our way.

Our seats were perfect—center stage and lower level. Mark and I sat with some of his fraternity brothers and their dates. It was about ten minutes before the concert was to begin, so the lights were still up. Excited laughter and speech filled the auditorium as people flowed in and found their seats.

I scanned the arena and saw another college group across the aisle, a couple of rows down. Several in the group were being noticeably loud and obnoxious.

I gasped as I spotted Nathan, who was drinking from a flask while draping his arm around the girl next to him.

Mark apparently heard me because he turned toward me, his eyebrows knitted. He followed the direction of my gaze.

"That's him, the one with the flask," I whispered.

Mark abruptly shifted in his seat to stand up. "I'll switch our seats with the last couple I just introduced you to. They're seated on the other end of our row."

"No, Mark. Seriously, let's keep our seats. I'm fine. I'm just concerned for his date."

I'd barely finished my sentence when the girl freed herself from Nathan's hold and, with a swaying stagger, made her way up the steps by grabbing on to the handrail.

I patted Mark's arm. "I'm going to follow her to make sure she's okay."

He nodded and went with me.

The girl had thick hair, the color of dark ginger, that bounced and glistened as she climbed the steps. She could have appeared in a Pantene commercial if it weren't for the wayward strands of hair straggling over her high cheekbones. With her bra strap hanging off her shoulder and her blouse partly unbuttoned, sadly, she was a mess. Despite her disheveled appearance, she radiated ethereal beauty.

She placed the palm of her hand over her mouth and rushed toward the women's restroom.

"Mark, I'm going to follow her in."

"All right. I'll wait outside the door here. Call me if you need me."

Rounding the corner, I saw her holding on to the swinging door of an open stall. She swayed forward and vomited into the toilet. I lunged to her and held her hair away from her face. I noticed other girls staring and whispering. I quietly closed the stall door behind us.

She was clearly undone as she heaved, vomited and sobbed almost simultaneously.

"I should get you medical assistance."

"No, please! I'm so embarrassed." She stopped talking to heave again then wiped her mouth. "Sorry, I didn't mean to raise my voice."

As I patted her on the back, she moaned. "I don't know what happened. My date gave me a Sprite and I became dizzy. I think I blacked out in the limo on the way over here. He must have slipped something in . . ." She heaved again, yet it seemed she had nothing left. She placed her delicate hands on her slender neck.

I pulled a bottle of water from my purse and handed it to her. She thanked me and took small sips. She pressed the cold bottle against her forehead.

When she seemed more stable, I led her to a bench near the restroom exit where there was better ventilation. I could hear music and cheering. The concert had begun.

She looked down at her blouse, sighing at the unfastened buttons. With trembling fingers, she refastened them. A tear dropped on her blouse. She looked up at me, tears pooling from her wide eyes onto her flawless skin. "I can't let my date take me home. I don't trust him."

"I agree. My date and I can take you home if you'd like. He's waiting right outside the restroom, but only when you feel ready to go. I promise, you can trust us to get you home safely."

She squinted, scrutinizing me through tears that caught on her long lashes. "Why . . . why would you do that?"

"Honestly? If I were in your predicament, I would want someone to help me. In fact, others have helped me when I've been in a similar situation. It's time I pay it forward. By the way, I'm Leah Morris. My date's name is Mark Taylor. We're freshmen here at UT."

"My name is Sarah. Thank you for helping me. Seriously, this has never happened to me before! I would feel safer if I got a ride home with you. But I don't want to ruin your date night. I'll just stay in here until the concert is over. That way you and your date can see the performance."

"We can leave now or whenever you're ready. You need to get home so you can rest. Will there be someone there who can stay with you until you feel better?"

"Yes, my roommate didn't have a date tonight, so she's there. We live at Kinsolving dorm. But I really don't want to put you out."

"Listen, I wouldn't have offered if I didn't want to help."

She paused, searching my eyes. "Okay. I'm ready to go."

When we joined Mark, he held out a cold water bottle to each of us. Sarah had regained some coloring and was walking more steadily.

Mark ran ahead to bring the car around to the center's entrance. I helped Sarah into the back seat.

She clenched her purse to her chest. "I'm so sorry for all the trouble."

Mark glimpsed in the rearview mirror. "No trouble at all. We're glad to help."

Once on the road, Mark looked over at me. He murmured, "At the concession across from the restrooms, security had Nathan cuffed and was escorting him out of the building." He spoke so low, Sarah couldn't possibly have heard.

Yet, she must have had superhuman hearing because she sat forward. "What? Wait! Did you say Nathan?"

I looked back at her. "Yes, your date tonight. I know Nathan because I dated him for a short time. It was a regretfully bad experience for me, kind of like what you went through tonight. When I saw you with him, I told Mark that I was concerned for your safety. That's why I followed you into the restroom—to make sure you were all right."

Sarah slumped back on the car's leather seat and slowly shook her head. "But why would you be so kind to me? I'm a stranger to you. Why would you miss the biggest concert of the year to be with me while I threw up?"

"When I saw you with Nathan, you reminded me of me at the beginning of this semester. I never want anyone to go through what I did." Mark reached over and held my hand. "A lot of people have helped me out, including Mark."

"I don't know what would have happened to me if you two hadn't come along. You saved me from a disastrous outcome."

"No, I believe God saved you. We were just privileged to be agents of His protection."

"It doesn't surprise me that you're a believer! Have you found a church here in Austin yet? I haven't."

"Yes, the campus community church just around the block. We go to the nine o'clock service."

"I haven't been there. Maybe I'll see you tomorrow."

Pulling up to the dorm entrance, Mark caught me in a glance as he spoke to Sarah. "Do you want to take Leah's cell number so you can give us a call when you make it to your room?"

I gave her my cell number then we said goodbye.

Mark parallel parked in front of the dorm, and we waited for her call.

I looked at Mark. "You are incredible. Thank you for helping others so selflessly."

"I was going to say the same thing about you, but you beat me to it. If I'm going to get to hang out with you, I really need to step up my game."

He placed his palm on my jaw and drew close. But before his lips touched mine, my phone buzzed. "Hi, Leah. It's Sarah. I made it to my room without falling on my face. Thank you, and please thank Mark, for everything! I'm so sorry for all the trouble. See you at church tomorrow."

"We were just glad to help. Looking forward to seeing you in the morning, Sarah."

I leaned over and kissed Mark's cheek. "Will you sing me a Garth Brooks song?"

"I can do better than that." He popped in a Garth Brooks CD and we drove away, singing at the top of our lungs.

20

In the morning, Mark and I spotted Sarah with another girl entering the church building. She introduced the girl as her roommate, Nicole.

Nicole's shiny jet-black hair framed her wide cheekbones and dark almond-shaped eyes. She stood about a foot shorter than Sarah.

"After Sarah described how you two took such good care of her last night, I just had to meet you." Nicole's voice was soft and slightly high-pitched with a staccato rhythm. Her cheeks rose in a smile.

We introduced Sarah and Nicole to others in the lobby, which was humming with conversations. They sat with us for the sermon, a continuation of the study of Luke.

Pastor David read the opening text from Luke 14:12–14, in which Jesus instructed, "When you give a dinner or a banquet, do not invite your friends or your brothers or your relatives or rich neighbors, lest they also invite you in return and you be repaid. But when you give a feast, invite the poor, the crippled, the lame, the blind, and you will be blessed, because they cannot repay you. For you will be repaid at the resurrection of the just."

I reflected on Jesus's instruction. Brooke had never expected any kind of repayment for all that she'd done for me. I was yearning to show the same depth of kindness to Sarah. *Lord, please give me the opportunity to serve You by being a support to Sarah.*

When the service ended, I reached for Mark's hand. "Would you be okay with Sarah and Nicole joining us for breakfast?"

He smiled. "I think that's a great idea. How about I ask people from our community group to join us too?"

"Sounds good." I squeezed his hand.

"After last night, I'm thinking Sarah may need Christian friends here on campus."

I pondered his words. I remembered telling Brooke I needed Christian friends when she befriended me.

Mark went over to some of our community group members while I turned my attention to Sarah and Nicole. "Would you guys like to grab breakfast with us?"

They accepted my offer about the time Mark came back with Abbey, John, and Brooke. We all headed out to Cisco's, a great hole-in-the-wall spot for migas and breakfast tacos.

The restaurant reverberated with the chatter of patrons and the clanging of dishes. Brooke had to raise her voice when she asked Sarah and Nicole how long they'd been attending the campus church.

"Today was our first time," Sarah said.

Brooke smiled. "Oh! How did you hear about our church?"

Sarah glanced at me then seemed to carefully chose her words. "Mark and Leah invited me when they dropped me off at my dorm last night. My date wound up being obnoxiously rude, and I was stranded, without a ride back to the dorm."

Brooke sighed. "Ugh! I think most of us have had at least one bad experience with an obnoxious date."

As the waitress came to take our orders, Mark and I exchanged glances. He was probably thinking what I was thinking: *Brooke, if you only knew you're referring to the same obnoxious guy.*

Abbey scooted her chair forward and leaned in. "So, Sarah and Nicole, what did y'all think about the church service this morning?"

Nicole beamed. "Loved it! Sarah and I were talking earlier about how it reminded us of our fellowship with people from our church back home."

John draped his arm on the back of Abbey's chair. "Where's home?"

"We're from Conroe. Our families live a couple of docks apart on the lake," Sarah said.

Nicole chuckled. "Yeah, we learned to water ski before we learned to jump rope."

Everyone eagerly shared personal experiences about water skiing. Brooke caught my eye and raised her eyebrows. I nodded at her and mouthed, *Yes, Nathan's Conroe*. After the waitress served our plates, we bowed our heads in a prayer of thanks.

At the end of breakfast, Abbey invited Sarah and Nicole to join community group. "We meet in the home of our leaders, Michael and Caroline Pate, on Thursday nights. All of us here go and there are others who, I know, would like to meet you. The only thing is, we don't start back up until January because of finals and Christmas break."

"That'd be great!" Sarah and Nicole said almost in unison.

"I'm so glad y'all will be joining us." Brooke said.

As we strolled out to our cars, Sarah pulled me aside. "Thank you for not telling the others of my embarrassing situation last night. I didn't sleep at all, worrying about what everyone who saw me in that condition must think of me now," she said in a hushed tone.

Buttoning my jacket, I looked over at Sarah and studied her expression. She appeared pensive and worried. "What happened was not your fault. You were the victim."

"I know but all the people who saw me will think I willingly got drunk or high." She pulled the collar of her jacket around her slender neck.

I reflected on my own shame and fear of how others viewed me. "I can relate, but I'm coming to realize that it doesn't matter what people think of us or how they see us. Whether it's a mistake we made or a wrong done to us, what really matters is how God sees us—how He sees our hearts."

Sarah's wide eyes scanned the parking lot, shifting her gaze from one person to another. She folded her arms tightly around her upper body and sighed heavily.

I lowered my voice. "Would it be all right if we meet somewhere near campus this afternoon so we can talk some more?"

She nodded slowly. "I'd like that."

Hours later, I stood in front of Sarah's dorm. She emerged from the entry, stopping on the steps to glance around until she spotted me. Before she could move forward, another girl, sprinting toward the entrance, ran into Sarah. Shoulders collided and Sarah wobbled sideways. "Oh, sorry," Sarah offered. The girl didn't give any notice, just raced past her.

Walking to Pease Park, I brought up the incident. "I couldn't help notice that you apologized to that girl who clearly ran into you. Hopefully, your shoulder isn't dislocated."

"I'm fine. I tend to apologize a lot." She raised her soft brows and shrugged.

I didn't tell her that I'd noticed. We shared our interests and a little bit about our pasts.

She held her sports bottle tightly, flipping the bottle cap back and forth. "I can't imagine how hard it must be for you, being so far from home. I'm only three hours from home, yet I feel like I'm light-years away."

As we walked, I learned that Sarah was close to her older brother, who attended A&M University, and her parents were devoted to them and their church.

Once we'd arrived at the park, we sat on the lawn in the shade of a huge oak tree overlooking Shoal Creek. A gentle breeze swept leaves onto a nearby running trail. Runners and bikers rushed past, focused on their journey. Otherwise, we were alone.

Sarah drew her knees toward her chest and hugged her legs. Her face was solemn. "I like being home with my family where I know I'm safe and accepted. Have you seen that new movie *Mean Girls*?"

I nodded.

"Well, there were some mean girls at my high school. They must have sensed my insecurities because they came after me big-time, smearing my reputation with false rumors to the extent that my prom date backed out on me."

"That's horrible!"

"My saving grace was Nicole. She stuck by me through it all. It's a wonder I still graduated with honors because I couldn't sleep, much less concentrate on my studies. The gossip was so widespread, Nicole and I weren't invited to any of the senior parties. We pretty much became recluses over the summer. My home was my shelter." Sarah drank from her sports bottle.

I pictured in my mind Sarah's home and the peace that she'd experienced with her family and best friend. So different from the home I'd escaped when moving away to college. "It's such a blessing that you had the support of Nicole and your family in the shelter of your home."

"Yeah, but Dad would remind me that our shelter isn't from our house, it's from God. Dad would quote Psalm forty-six verse one, 'God is our refuge and strength, a very present help in trouble.' Mom would point to the plaque she has hanging in our kitchen: 'He who dwells in the shelter of the Most High will abide in the shadow of the Almighty.' It's Psalm ninety-one verse one."

"Your parents sound amazing!"

She looked at me with sad eyes and a brittle smile. "I know. I miss them. But it wasn't always that way. Mom had me in all sorts of clubs and competitions, and I think she got caught up in living through my activities. She was all about appearances. It seemed important to her that my cheerleading uniform fit just right, and my hair looked just so. When the mean girls went after me, she turned to her ladies Bible study for prayer. That's when I saw a total change in her. She stopped nagging me about my clothes and hair, and she started praying with Dad."

"You know, I think those girls were just jealous of your intelligence, your beauty, and your kind demeanor. You have so much going for you, and they probably wanted to elevate themselves by putting you down."

"You're sweet for encouraging me. But now I fear that I'm the one caught up on appearances and what people think. I was hoping that Nathan hadn't heard the rumors from home and he'd just asked me out because he was interested in me. He seemed sincere because of the nice things he'd said to me. But the way he treated me last night, I'm sure he had heard the gossip and asked me out only because he believed the rumors. Really? I hardly know how to talk to guys, much less. . ." Sarah rolled her eyes then held her gaze downward.

I tucked my feet under my legs, shifting to lean toward her. "Our stories are very similar and with the same villain. I thought Nathan cared for me. On our last date, he spiked my drink and I passed out overnight."

I didn't mention that I'd found myself in Nathan's bed the next morning or that I'd become pregnant, because I didn't think the news would be helpful at that point. It would have probably added to her grief. As our friendship grew, I would tell her. *Lord, help me to become a wise mentor to Sarah. I'm so ill-equipped.*

I reached into my backpack and pulled out the Bible Brooke had given me.

Sarah and I read several verses that I had tabbed about trying to please people rather than God.

Sarah read aloud the last one: Galatians 1:10. "For am I now seeking the approval of man, or of God? Or am I trying to please man? If I were still trying to please man, I would not be a servant of Christ." Sarah brushed her delicate hand across the page. She slowly closed the Bible and handed it to me. "I never saw the personal implications in those verses until now. I guess I've wandered so far from the Lord. It's true, I care more about what people think of me than what God thinks of me. I look at tons of fashion magazines and search the internet for the latest trends, but I don't think I've looked up one Bible verse since I've started college." She shook her head. "I don't even know if I brought my Bible to campus. How weird that I don't even know."

"I get what you're saying. I left my Bible buried in a storage bin at home when I came here. But I retrieved it when I went home recently." I held out the Bible to her. "You can have this one if you'd like."

"Really?" She cupped the Bible in her hands then drew it close. "I'll return it to you before we leave for Christmas break."

I waved my hand in the air. "No, I have my other one. I believe this one was meant to be passed on."

"Thank you." Her eyes sparkled.

"With this being finals week, how about we call each other daily to share Scripture." I tilted my head. "Would you have the time?"

"I'll make the time. That would mean a lot to me!"

21

Yes! I was finished with finals, and I was exhausted. I stared up at the ceiling. This dorm mattress never felt so comfy. It had been a stressful week, but I thought I had done well on all my exams.

I got out of bed and sat in front of the mirror to check my hair. I was startled by my reflection. I looked like the porcelain doll that Mom kept on the closet shelf during my childhood. As I applied blush, not just to my cheeks, but to my forehead and chin, I reflected on the past several days. I'd talked with Sarah every night that week. Between studying for finals, we'd studied what the Bible stated about our identity in Christ. I'd been humbled and, at the same time, honored to be called a daughter of my almighty God. I was beginning to see my worth and purpose as God intended. I hoped Sarah was as well.

My thoughts were interrupted by my phone ringing.

"Hey, Mark!"

"Hey, babe! You ready?"

"Absolutely! I'll be down in a second."

Mark and I were going out to dinner to celebrate the completion of finals. He'd made reservations at a popular Italian restaurant. I'd never been there, but I'd heard it was amazing.

As we drove off, Mark smiled at me. "Your face has a beautiful glow, but you look a little pale, babe. How did your day go?"

"I'm glowing because I have a date with the most handsome guy on campus." I sighed. "I won't sugar-coat it. My day was exhausting. You're probably as thankful as I am that finals are finally over."

"You have a doctor's check-up next week, right?"

"Yeah, Monday. It's a good thing. I had some mild cramping last night and this morning, but I'm sure it was just brought on by the stress of the week."

Mark's eyes darted at mine and a crease appeared between his brows. "How are you feeling now?"

"I'm all right."

"You're sure?"

"Yes."

"Would it be all right if I took you to the appointment Monday?"

"I'd love that."

We arrived at the restaurant and Mark dropped me off at the entrance then parked the car.

I walked up to the hostess. "We have a reservation for Taylor, party of two."

"Certainly, Mrs. Taylor. We'll be calling you shortly."

Without bothering to correct her, I sat on a bench in the foyer.

Mark walked in and sat beside me. His jaw and shoulder muscles were tense. "Leah, are you sure you're all right?"

"I'll be fine. Please relax. I probably just need to eat something."

The hostess approached. "Your table is ready. This way, please."

Mark placed his arm around my waist as we followed her.

The waiter set garlic bread and glasses of water on our table. "I'll return when you've had a chance to look at the menu."

I tried to focus on the soft piano music and the delightful aromas of Italian herbs and spices. I sipped the water, hoping it would refresh me.

The cramping worsened. I shifted in my chair, trying to gain some measure of comfort. I winced with another twinge.

"What can I do, Leah?"

"I'm okay. I'm just going to go freshen up in the ladies' room."

Once there, I was alarmed to find blood on my undergarment.

I returned to our table and told Mark.

"I'm taking you to the hospital." He ran out to pull the car to the entrance then returned to help me to the door.

We made it to the ER in record time.

They put me into an exam room that smelled like a combination of Pine-Sol and Listerine. Mark stood by my side as a nurse took my temperature.

The doctor entered, flipping through a chart. Then he looked up at me. "Leah Morris?"

"Yes."

"Hello, I'm Dr. Harris." He flashed a smile at Mark and me. "I read on your intake form that you're pregnant. How far along are you?"

"Sixteen weeks."

"What brings you to the ER tonight? Describe your symptoms."

"I've been experiencing some mild cramping that started last night and continued on and off today. This evening, the cramping increased, and within the last hour, I realized I was spotting."

He asked me numerous follow-up questions while the nurse continued to check my vital signs. I noticed my breathing was rapid, so I was sure my blood pressure was elevated. The doctor became silent as he placed the chest piece of his stethoscope over my heart.

He flipped the earpieces of the stethoscope around his neck and propelled his rolling stool to the desk. He jotted some notes on a pad of paper then said, "All right. I've ordered an ultrasound. Once that is completed, I'll be back to examine you. Do you have any questions for me at this point?"

"No, not right now."

He nodded and left the room.

My heart fluttered. I stared at Mark. He reached for my hand, then kissed it.

The technician burst into the room, hustling to set up the equipment.

Mark caressed my hand. "I'm going to be right down the hall praying. Remember, God is in control."

I nodded.

He gently kissed my forehead then left the room.

After I underwent over an hour of procedures and exams, I was relieved to have Mark by my side again.

He held my hand. "How are you doing?"

"Good." I forced a smile.

Dr. Harris entered. Mark remained close to me.

The doctor cleared his throat and looked back and forth at Mark and me. "The ultrasound looked good. The baby's size and position appear normal. No structural abnormalities were detected. Both baby and mother appear healthy." He stood with his legs apart, both feet firmly planted on the vinyl floor. "The cramping may have been due to stress or fatigue. Have you been under added stress lately?"

"Yes, I have."

"That may explain the bleeding. The results of the blood work are pending so we'll send those to your regular obstetrician." He adjusted his glasses and skimmed my chart. "It's Dr. Tullos, correct?"

"That's correct."

He nodded slowly. "I am ordering bed rest until you're able to see Dr. Tullos."

"I have an appointment scheduled with her on Monday. But on Wednesday I'm to fly out to New York to spend Christmas with my mom."

He shook his head. "No travel unless you clear it with Dr. Tullos." He addressed Mark. "She must get as much rest as possible."

Mark squeezed my hand, graced me with a reassuring smile, and put his arm around me. "I'll take good care of her, Doctor."

Relieved that the baby seemed fine, I felt like myself again. I was also starving.

Mark ordered take-out from the Italian restaurant we had abruptly left earlier. We arrived right before they closed and picked up the order. He then drove us to a little bakery that stayed open late. It had a secluded balcony with a small wrought iron table and chairs overlooking Town Lake. He'd already called ahead to the bakery, making sure they'd allow us to eat our Italian take-out if we ordered their dessert.

It was the perfect evening with a mild, cool breeze. I adjusted my thin scarf around my neck.

Mark pulled my chair out for me, and I lowered myself into the seat. "This night air, Mark! It's refreshing. Back home, I'm certain no one is sitting out on a patio. Right now, New York is covered in snow."

"Well, this sixty-eight-degree temperature is nice, but next week it'll drop back into the forties. Typical Texas weather. He draped his jacket around my shoulders and sat close. The warmth of his jacket and the closeness of his body wrapped me in a cocoon of protection.

The full moon reflecting off the lake completed our romantic setting.

When we had enjoyed every bite, including dessert, Mark cleared his throat and shifted in his chair to face me. I admired every feature of his kind face.

"Leah, tonight, when I realized you and the baby might be in danger, I thought I'd lose my mind. I was crazy with worry. I know we've been dating only a short time, but I need to tell you, I love you."

My heart pounded so fiercely; it wouldn't have surprised me if it leaped from my chest. "I love you too, Mark. I've known it from the first moment we studied the Bible together."

He sighed and touched his forehead to mine. After a moment, he cupped my face in his strong hands. "I realize our relationship is just beginning but, if you'll have me, I want to spend the rest of my life with you. I want to marry you one day and be a godly father to the baby."

I closed my eyes and buried my face into his chest. No way could I stop the tears from flowing.

He lifted my face to his and kissed me tenderly. He then gazed into my eyes.

"I need to get you back to the dorm so you can rest—doctor's orders." He winked and flashed a smile that radiated warmth.

How could I possibly sleep after all that Mark and I had said to each other?

22

"The baby's heartbeat is strong, and the growth is well within normal limits. Everything looks normal, including your blood work."

Mark and I audibly exhaled in synchrony. He wrapped his arm around me.

"I'm so thankful the baby is thriving, Dr. Tullos." I couldn't keep the tremble from my voice. "After my scare Friday night, having this appointment booked with you for almost a month was a godsend."

"I agree, Leah. I'm seeing patients back-to-back today since our office will be closed for the holidays starting tomorrow."

She turned the ultrasound monitor so we could see the baby.

Mark pointed at the screen and spoke through laughter, "Oh, wow! Look at the baby's little features! Look at the ears and mouth. . .with full lips, just like yours, Leah!"

Joy didn't come close to describing what I was feeling!

Dr. Tullos smiled. "Would you like to know the gender?"

Mark and I exchanged looks, raised our eyebrows, and nodded to each other.

"Is that a yes?" She must have needed a verbal confirmation.

"Yes," we said.

"It's a girl."

"Oh, Mark!" I grabbed his hand. Tears welled in my eyes.

As many times as I'd seen Mark smile, I'd never seen such a wide and beaming one. He leaned over and kissed my forehead. "We're going to have a little girl!"

"Congratulations, you two!" Doctor Tullos's eyebrows raised, wrinkling her forehead. "Now, Leah, you must try to get as much rest as possible."

"I will. I've rearranged my holiday plans. Rather than flying home to New York, my mom is flying here."

When I had called mom to tell her of the bleeding and the ER doctor's instruction that I not fly, she insisted on coming to see me. I was grateful that the Pates had offered their garage apartment for mom's visit. I would be staying with her for the holiday.

Mark's parents invited us to dinner that evening. This was just my fifth time to see them, but Mark and I had decided it was time to tell them of my pregnancy. At first, this seemed bizarre to me. But Mark reassured me that his parents would be accepting. He reminded me that the longer we waited to share the news, the harder it would be.

Mark held my hand as we entered their home. His touch helped to calm me somewhat, but telling your boyfriend's parents that you're pregnant with another man's child was sure to be a shocker. Thankfully, the temperatures had plummeted into the low forties that evening, allowing me to wear layers of sweaters to hide my baby bump until we'd had the chance to tell them. Mark also suggested that we wait until after dinner, which also seemed bizarre. *Before I drop a bomb on you, Mr. and Mrs. Taylor, let me dine at your table.*

The food and conversation were wonderful, though I found it difficult to eat much since my stomach twisted in tension. Mark's sister, Hannah, was out with friends, so it was just the four of us.

When everyone had finished eating, Mark placed his napkin on the table and leaned forward. "Mom, thank you for a wonderful meal."

"Yes, Mrs. Taylor, everything was delicious." As I spoke, Mark reached for my hand.

"It gave me such joy to prepare it." Mrs. Taylor's eyes gleamed in the same way that Mark's did when he seemed happiest.

Mark cleared his throat. "Leah and I appreciate you both having us for dinner. I want you to know that I respect and care for Leah a great deal."

Mr. Taylor leaned back in his chair, bracing himself with the arm-rests as he exploded in a lighthearted laugh. "Well, Mark, you've only been talking about Leah since the day you met her." He grinned mischievously. "Oops, was I not supposed to mention that?"

Mark rolled his eyes and smiled. "Thanks for sharing, Dad. But seriously, Leah and I have decided you need to know something. It's something for which we've both been in prayer"

Please help, Lord. "Mr. and Mrs. Taylor, thank you for raising such a wonderful son. I'm so blessed by Mark."

I dreaded how their smiles would fade as soon as I shared my news. I was so thankful Mark's sister wasn't there—one less face to reflect disappointment.

Heartbreaking how one wrong decision can adversely affect so many people.

They knew that Mark and I had met at church, so I started my story with what happened before Mark and I met. *This is tough!*

I began slowly. "Before I met Mark, I was dating a senior on campus who I thought at the time was sincere about the feelings he expressed for me. One night, I accepted a soda from him. As I drank it, I became light-headed, but I continued drinking. That turned out to be the worst decision I've ever made. At some point that night, I blacked out, though I have no recall of it happening."

My words came out stifled. I lowered my head, swallowed hard, then looked up, steeling myself for the displeasure that was sure to come when I revealed the rest of my story.

My voice was barely audible. "Now I'm pregnant with that man's child."

No one spoke. No one moved. Only dead silence. I couldn't find my breath . . . but I found immense comfort in Mark's nearness as he continued to grasp my hand.

Mr. Taylor broke the silence. "It sounds like date rape. Have you filed charges?"

"Leah has prayed earnestly about all of this. She's going to keep the baby and no charges will be filed, at least not right now."

"But, son, what if this man tries this with other young women?" Mr. Taylor tossed his napkin on the table and leaned forward.

That was the exact possibility that had been haunting me for a while. I bit my lip and looked down at Mark's hand steadying mine.

"That's a great point, Dad. Just so you know, Leah and I saw this man recently at a concert, and his date seemed to be in a similar situation as Leah had been. What are the odds, except through God's provision? With Leah's discernment, we were able to intervene on the girl's behalf and connect her with our friends at church. Without Leah's care and concern, that wouldn't have happened. Also, I witnessed the man being hand-cuffed and escorted out of the concert hall that night so, hopefully, that will put a stop to his future offenses."

Mrs. Taylor pushed back her chair, rose, and rushed to embrace me. "My dear, I admire you for keeping the baby. That speaks volumes about you and your faith."

I looked at her through my tears. My voice quivered. "Mrs. Taylor, thank you for that! God surrounded me with Christians who've shared the gospel and prayed with me. Mark has been among those who've supported me. God has been relentless in providing for me and the baby . . . in extraordinary ways."

Mr. Taylor raised his brows. "It sounds like this baby is a testimony of love." He spoke it in a sincere tone, but deep lines appeared on his forehead as he studied Mark.

Mark nodded. "Yes, Dad, a testimony of God's love and the love that Leah and I have for each other."

Mark and I locked eyes. I've never felt more connected to someone as I did at that moment.

Of course, Mark's dad wanted to know if we'd thought through the details and what would happen next. He was pretty much like most dads, wanting to know the plan.

Thankfully, Mark took over. "Leah accepted a part-time babysitting position from the couple who leads our Bible-study group. Her dorm and meals are paid up through the spring semester. When the baby arrives, Leah will move into the couple's garage apartment and the wife of the couple will share the babysitting responsibilities of their two children and this baby. That will allow Leah to continue school and graduate on time. Leah's mom will be paying any tuition that Leah's wages don't cover."

Mark paused, seeming to weigh his next words. "Dad, what I'm about to say will be difficult to understand. But I've told Leah, and I'm telling you both now, despite the short time we've been dating, I want to one day marry Leah and be the adoptive father to this child."

I glanced between Mr. and Mrs. Taylor. My head was spinning. Mark's parents were calm. *Unbelievable! How am I keeping my dinner down?*

We talked around the table for a while, discussing a multitude of subjects: Mark and me, our situation, our plans, and, most importantly, God's provision.

At a lull in the conversation, Mrs. Taylor began clearing the dishes from the table. I jumped up to gather plates and follow her into the kitchen. I moved to the sink and began rinsing the plates.

Mrs. Taylor put her hand on my shoulder. "You don't have to help with this. I was just clearing the dishes to get them off the table and out of our way."

"It would give me such joy if you'd let me help."

Her mouth stretched into a smile that reached her eyes. "Well, all right, dear. Thank you."

I began stacking the rinsed plates on the counter. "Mrs. Taylor, I need for you to know that I respect and honor Mark, and the last thing I want to do is hurt him. Of course, these circumstances are a horrible way to start a relationship. When I first met Mark, I didn't know I was pregnant."

"I believe you're sincere. I've never seen Mark look at a girl like he looks at you. It's obvious he cares a great deal for you."

"I care a great deal for him. Before I agreed to go on an official date with him, I told him of my pregnancy. Mark was so amazing; he still wanted to take me out."

My vision blurred, despite rapid blinking to hold back the tears.

"I'm so glad to hear that the news didn't cause my son to change his mind about dating you. It's apparent that you two belong together." Mrs. Taylor placed her elbows on the kitchen counter and leaned into her forearms. "I'm just sorry that the other situation came about, and you were deceived. I can't imagine how awful it's been for you."

"I'm sorry too. I never dreamed I'd find myself in this situation. But because of my wrong choice and wanting to be accepted by a man who, I've come to realize, never had my interest at heart, I need to make the right choice now. I want to honor God and raise this baby to learn about Him."

"Many families encounter unexpected, difficult situations that change the course of their lives. I'm astonished by the faith instilled in you, Leah. God will be faithful to see you through."

"Thank you, Mrs. Taylor. Mark keeps reassuring me of that. I'm grateful that you and Mr. Taylor trained him up to love God." I clasped my hands under my chin.

She gently touched my arm. "I know your mom lives in New York. Please know I'm here if ever you need anything—support, a safe-haven, a hug."

We hugged each other. *Thank You, gracious God!*

Driving back with Mark to campus, my mind replayed my conversation with Mark's mom. She was unbelievably gracious, especially after being told that her son was in love with a pregnant woman.

Mark interrupted my thoughts. "Hey, babe, are you all right? You look deep in thought."

"You know, you're right. I'm thinking about your sweet mom . . . how she unconditionally accepted me. I think it's because she sees how deeply you care for me."

"Well, I'm hoping my obvious love for you has something to do with it, but I have to also believe that her love for the Lord takes precedence over that. Mom has a way of discerning a person's character. I recognized her ability to do this during my high school years. She wisely let me know when I was hanging out with the good, the bad, and the ugly. Sorry, I'm a Clint Eastwood fan."

I laughed. "I love you! I was so blessed by your mom's response. She said to me in the kitchen tonight that all families have unexpected situations that change the course of their lives. You've told me your parents are actively involved in church. Is your mom connected to some sort of family ministry?"

"She's in a ministry at their church that supports people in need. But I'm certain she was referring to our own family history." Mark stopped at a red light and looked at me with those blue eyes that touched my soul. "My parents adopted Hannah from one of my mom's cousins who was considering aborting her in the first trimester. Hannah knows she's adopted. My parents explained to her, when she was old enough to understand, that she was wanted and loved by them before she was even born. Hannah realizes that she was chosen, just like God chooses us as adopted sons and daughters through our faith in Jesus."

The light turned green and, as Mark accelerated the car, I pondered his words. Finally, I said, "Has Hannah ever met her biological mother?"

"Yes, and after the second visit, the mother became unavailable. Hannah considers my mom her real mom."

Mark pulled up in front of my dorm and turned off the engine.

"You and your family are incredible. I'm so thankful you're in my life."

"I'm so thankful you're in mine, Leah. I want to take care of you if you'll let me. I was able to get a full-time job at ACE hardware for the holidays. They'll keep me on part-time once school resumes. I also got the TA position in the School of Architect. With the money I'll earn, I can at least start helping you buy baby supplies and furniture."

"Mark, you don't—"

"Yes, I do. I want to."

"I don't know what to say!"

"Just say that you'll let me help. That you'll keep me in your life."

My cheeks were moist with tears. "I will."

Mark tenderly kissed away my tears.

23

Mark and I picked up Mom from the airport Wednesday morning. Mom and Mark hit it off right away. I hardly got a word in. They talked nonstop and acted like they'd known each other forever. I couldn't have been more thankful.

We stopped at one of our favorite restaurants for brunch. I had to admit, I was feeling a little left out as they connected in a deep conversation that spanned a wide range of topics, all to which they agreed. They interacted almost like mother and son. We ended up staying at our table for so long, Mark gave our waiter more than just a generous tip.

As Mark drove us to the Pate's garage apartment, I brought up Christmas day. "I was telling Mom about your mom's sweet invitation to spend Christmas evening with them."

"That reminds me. Mom wanted me to ask if five o'clock Christmas evening would work for you."

"Yes, five would be great. Right, Mom?"

"Absolutely wonderful!"

From the moment she arrived, Mom had been upbeat and talkative, the mom I had known from my childhood. It warmed my heart!

Oh, the thrill of Christmas morning! Mom and I were sipping eggnog and enjoying her homemade quiche. We decided to spend quiet time together before going downstairs to visit the Pates.

I put on Christmas music, and Mom and I exchanged gifts. Mom gave me an infant swaddling blanket and a nursing robe, both in a matching floral print. I teared up, and it wasn't just because of my hormones. She teared up too when she opened my gift to her, a Christmas ornament that read: "Grandma Est. 2005."

"Honey, I hope to be the kind of grandma to the baby that my mom was to you."

"Mom, your being who you are and being here now proves that you already are an amazing grandma. Thank you for being here for me and the baby; it means the world."

Mom seemed at a loss for words as she embraced me, and we shared a quiet, emotional moment.

Time with the Pates was wonderful. Mom and I enjoyed watching Becca and Zeke open their Christmas gifts. We bought them a Noah's ark toy and some children's books. I was touched by the pure joy that emulated from Mom's eyes as she watched the kids' play with their new toys.

Around ten o'clock, Brooke texted me: *Call me when you can.*

I moved to a quiet corner of the Pate's home and called her. "Hey, Brooke! Merry Christmas!"

"Aw, Merry Christmas to you! I've been thinking about you. How are you?"

"I'm good. Mom is here and we just opened gifts. How are you guys?"

"We're good! John just proposed to Abbey out on the deck. Complete surprise! Well, at least for all of us . . . maybe not for Abbey. They're looking at next December for the wedding."

"Oh, wow! You guys must be over the moon with joy! Please send my congratulations to everyone!"

"I will. It sounds like you have a lot of excitement there!"

"Yeah, Becca and Zeke are playing with their new toys. They've just found me in my secluded corner. They're looking at me with their big eyes that are begging, 'Play with us!' They're adorable!"

"They are awesome kids! I won't keep you, I just wanted you to know that I'm thinking about you and praying that you and your mom have a wonderful Christmas Day together."

"Thank you so much. Mom and I are having dinner with Mark and his family later. I know that it will be great, but prayers, please."

"You got it. You sound so happy."

"Yeah. God is good!"

"All the time! 'Bye, Leah."

"See you later."

Christmas with Mark and his family was way more incredible than I'd expected. As we stepped into the Taylors' home, they welcomed us with open arms. Mom offered hosting gifts—a crystal candy dish and chocolates. I could tell she was nervous by the way her hand trembled as she offered them.

"Thank you so much. This candy dish is lovely!" Mrs. Taylor hugged Mom.

"And the chocolates look like they need to be sampled right now." Mr. Taylor gave his sneaky grin and reached for the box.

Mrs. Taylor tightened her grasp on the gift. "They're for dessert, darlin'."

Mom laughed quietly, her shoulders relaxing with each chuckle. Her laughter mixed with ours.

Once we were seated at the table, Mr. Taylor prayed, thanking God for His many blessings. Throughout dinner, the mood was comfortable and the conversation upbeat. Truly, God was in control.

After dinner, Mark said, "Mrs. Morris, may I show you the view from the patio before the sun completely sets?"

"I've been dying to get a better glimpse of that view." Mom followed Mark onto the patio, turning her head peripherally to scan the hillside. From my vantage point inside, I could see the skyline, lit up with countless shades of orange and red and capped with hovering clouds that accentuated the vivid colors across the sky. I could see Mark talking to her. After finishing her scan of the horizon, she nodded in his direction.

Hannah jumped up and grabbed my hand. "Leah, come with me. I want you to see the clothes I got for Christmas!" She chattered all the way up the stairs. We stayed in her room for at least twenty minutes, picking out shoes to coordinate with her new outfits as she jabbered about her friends and school. She was quickly becoming the little sister I never had.

The clashing of dishes and Mr. Taylor's hearty laughter prompted us to head downstairs. Dessert was warm Texas Southern pecan pie made even more scrumptious by dollops of whipped cream.

Mom convinced the Taylors to save the chocolates for another day. "This delicious pie makes the evening perfectly complete."

After we said our goodbyes, Mark drove us back to the apartment in a round-about way to enjoy the yard decorations and Christmas lights displayed throughout the surrounding neighborhoods. I took in all the sights and relished that time with three of the most important people in my life: Mark, Mom, and my baby girl.

When Mom and I entered the apartment, she disappeared into the bedroom to change into her PJs. I took the time to call Sarah.

"Hey, Sarah! Merry Christmas! How are you?"

"Leah! Merry Christmas! Thank you so much for calling. Yeah, everything is great here. We're having the best time. I'm loving the family traditions that my parents and grandparents so meticulously arranged. How are you? How are Mark and your mom?"

"Great! We just got back from having a wonderful dinner with Mark's family. It's so good to hear your voice. I'm glad you and your family are enjoying Christmas traditions. I was just wondering how I might be praying for you."

"Well . . . just continued prayers, please, that I can find forgiveness in my heart for Nathan. Since I'm still harboring anger and resentment toward him, I'm hoping I won't run into him while I'm here in Conroe. But if I do, I want . . . I don't know, I want to react in a manner that honors the Lord."

"I'll be praying for that. Like you, after my bad experience with Nathan, I'm still trying to forgive him. I'm reminding myself daily that Jesus went to the cross to pay for my sins. Seriously, Jesus's sacrifice was so unbelievably more than what God calls me to do, to forgive the sins of others. I'm still struggling. When I feel myself becoming resentful, I recite to myself a verse from Ephesians four. 'Be kind to one another, tenderhearted, forgiving one another, as God in Christ forgave you.' It helps."

"Love it! That's gonna be my go-to verse. Seriously, Leah, I'm so grateful God placed you in my life! How can I pray for you?"

"Please pray that my mom has safe travel back to New York. She flies out Sunday afternoon. My time with her has been amazing."

"You got it. I can't wait to meet the rest of the community group when we get back. Thank you, Leah, for calling."

"The group is looking forward to meeting you and Nicole soon. I'm glad we were able to talk. Tell Nicole I said hi, and take care."

After we hung up, I couldn't stop thinking about Sarah. When she saw me after Christmas break, my pregnancy would be obvious. My baby bump, which had remained unnoticed under winter sweaters, will have turned into a baby belly. I needed to find the right time to tell her. For sure before our next community group meeting, since everyone else in the group knew. I didn't want her and Nicole to be blindsided.

Mom came out, face freshly washed, and PJs donned.

"Mom, do you remember my telling you about the girl that Mark and I helped at the concert?"

She nodded.

"I just got off the phone with her. I haven't yet told her that I'm pregnant. I feel like I've been misleading. But I just met her. How do I tell her since we don't know each other that well?"

Mom settled into the recliner and pulled her feet under her. "I wish your grandma were here to give you Bible verses. All I know is, God will be faithful and present. I'll be praying He'll give you the opportunity and the words to tell her. I'll also be praying Sarah will accept the news."

"Thank you!"

Gratitude filled me with how God had reunited me with mom, and at a time I needed her most.

"So, Mom, you and Mark have hit it off since the moment you arrived. You two looked like you were in a deep discussion on the balcony after dinner tonight."

She pulled a blanket over her legs and chuckled. "He couldn't stop talking about how he adores you."

Her words made me smile. "I adore him too."

"Yeah!" Mom's eyes lit up. "I can tell."

I jumped up to change into my PJs too. It was hot chocolate time!

24

I slept in the next day after all the Christmas fun and festivities. I was stepping out of the shower and slipping into my robe when my phone rang. I saw it was Mark and my heart leaped.

"Good morning, handsome! Thank you for dinner at your parents' last night. Mom and I had such a good time."

"Yeah, babe! It was a great evening with you and your mom. You doing all right this morning?"

"I am. So glad to have morning sickness days behind me. I was about to fix Mom's breakfast, but by the smell of bacon filling this apartment, I think she beat me to it." I peeked around the corner to see Mom busy in the kitchen. I caught her eye and we exchanged smiles. "When do you have to leave for work, Mark?"

"I'm leaving now and just noticed a plastic pill vial on the backseat. The label has your mom's name on it. Should I bring it to you now?"

I looked at Mom. "Mark's leaving for work and just saw your pill vial on his backseat. Do you need it now?"

"Oh! I'm so sorry. It must have fallen out of my purse last night. It's my blood pressure medicine." Her eyes widened and darted from side to side. "I don't need to take it until lunch or dinner. Could he drop it by after work?"

"Mark, did you hear that?"

"Yeah, I'd be happy to bring it to her this afternoon, especially since I'd be able to steal a kiss from you when I see you."

"Aw, you won't have to steal one. I'll gladly share all my kisses with you."

"I'll hold you to that! Hey, I know it's your last night with your mom, but if your mom isn't too sick of me yet, may I take you both to dinner when I come by?"

I turned to Mom. Clearly, she'd overheard because her eyes lit up as she nodded her head.

"Sure! We'd love it!"

"Great! I'll get there by four so your mom can get her medicine. I'll make reservations at that new restaurant on Lake Travis for five."

"That'll be wonderful! Be safe on your way to work, and we'll see you at four. Love you."

"I love you too, Leah."

I looked at Mom and tilted my head. "I didn't know you were on blood pressure medicine."

"I know." She wiped her hands on the dish towel. "My doctor told me I could get off the medicine if I started controlling my diet and exercising. I'll start taking better care of myself."

"Promise?"

She nodded. "Promise."

The day passed in a flash. At four o'clock, Mark arrived with Mom's medicine. Mom and Mark talked excitedly all the way to the restaurant.

The restaurant parking lot was packed. So was the dining room. I guessed we weren't the only ones who'd heard about this new five-star restaurant with "breathtaking views" of Lake Travis.

The hostess led us through the large dining room to a smaller room that had only about eight tables. We were the first party to be seated.

The room featured massive windows and tall French doors that opened to a private balcony overlooking the lake. The panoramic view encompassed foothills touching sparkling water that rippled with the wakes of motorboats speeding across the lake.

The hostess handed us our menus. "I apologize that the main dining room is full. We had to open up this smaller room to accommodate today's calls for reservations."

"I should have made my reservation before today. But, thank you. This is nice," Mark said.

I couldn't tear my eyes from the glorious sunset. "It's perfect!"

As we glanced over our menus, the waiter rattled off the specials. Once we'd ordered, Mom asked the waiter for directions to the ladies' room.

Mark and I slipped onto the balcony to take in the full view of the lake. The water seemed to dance as it glistened in the sunlight. I felt the soft warmth of the fading rays wash over my skin. The sun was brilliant with orange and red hues.

I looked up at Mark, his face glowed in the sunlight. "This is beautiful!"

"Leah, you are beautiful!" He pulled me close and kissed me softly.

I hoped Mom hadn't returned to our table to catch us in this private moment. I feared it would make her feel uncomfortable, like a third wheel.

Mark released me from our kiss. I opened my eyes and gasped. He was kneeling on one knee. He lifted his palm upward. In it rested a dazzling diamond ring. My hand flew to my mouth.

"Leah, will you marry me?"

My heart beat a rhythm of yes. Yes. Yes! I managed to speak. "Oh, Mark! Yes, I will!"

Mark put the most gorgeous, vintage-style, square-cut ring on my finger. I stared, mesmerized by its brilliance. He stood and wrapped me in his arms.

We kissed for what seemed like forever before we were interrupted with clapping and cheering. I spun around to see Brooke grinning from ear to ear.

"What? Brooke!"

"I wouldn't have missed this for the world! We took a road trip from Dallas today."

I looked around and saw a crowd of smiling faces. Maddi, Kara, Abbey, and John were beaming.

John said, "Yeah, I drove with four women from Dallas. I'm buying ear plugs for the trip home tomorrow."

Laughing, Abbey gently slapped his shoulder and John feigned pain.

"Aw, you guys!" I stepped forward and hugged my Dallas friends. "Abbey and John, congratulations on your engagement!"

To add to our joy, the Pates were there. Becca and Zeke broke loose from their parents' hold and ran to me. Mark snatched them up in his arms so they could hug my neck.

Mark's parents and my mom hugged me too.

"Mom, when did you find out?"

"Mark called me to ask my permission for your hand before I left New York. He was briefing me on the details of the plan last night on the balcony. Together, we schemed the medicine ploy. I hope you weren't worried about the medicine, honey."

Mark grinned mischievously. "I printed a fake prescription label and filled the vial with tic tacs. It provided an excuse to see you so I could get you here. I was nervous my plan would fall through."

I shook my head then kissed Mark on the cheek. "You went to a lot of trouble to arrange this!"

I held out my left hand. "Mom! Look at this ring! Oh, Mark, this ring! It's stunning!" I gripped his arm.

"It was my grandmother's. Mom has been saving it for me for this very day." He gestured toward his mom.

"Mrs. Taylor, this is exquisite! What a treasure to know it's a family heirloom."

Mrs. Taylor's eyes exuded genuine joy. "Leah, sweetheart, it's been saved just for you."

I embraced her again, lingering in the embrace with my eyes closed.

Hannah wrapped her arms around her mom and me. "Leah, do you know how hard it was for me to keep this secret? I can't tell you how many times I almost let it slip last night."

Mr. Taylor patted my shoulder. "Welcome to the family."

"Thank you, Mr. Taylor."

"Well, I'm hoping you'll drop the Mr. Taylor and call me Dad."

"Thanks, Dad!" I grinned.

Our attention was diverted to a couple of Mark's fraternity brothers slapping him on the back.

The one whose name was Jake asked, "Hey, man, what would you have done if she'd turned you down?"

"Yeah, I thought about that. Plan B would have been to jump into the lake."

"Oh, yeah, sure." Jake and some of the other guys roared.

The hostess appeared at the door. "Excuse me, sir. Your private room is now set up."

Mark beamed. "Thank you for playing along with my scheme." He looked down at me and winked.

I felt my eyes widening. "Are you kidding me? How long have you been planning this?"

"For what seems like forever, babe. The details? Weeks."

"How did I not see this coming? Everyone knew about this but me?" I eyed the family and friends that had gathered around us.

Everyone's hugs and laughter enveloped me. The crowd headed inside for dinner. Everyone but Mark and me.

I kissed Mark. "I will always treasure the memory of this night."

He cupped my chin. "I look forward to many more cherished memories that we'll build and share in our life together."

"Thank you for loving me so incredibly well."

"Thank you for the honor of having you as my beautiful bride."

Jake came to the door. "Hey, you two, I finished off your salads. It's okay if I start on your entrees, right?"

Mark rolled his eyes. We laughed and followed Jake inside.

III

PART

Sarah

25

December 2004
Conroe, Texas

"Sarah, why didn't you call me to ask me about Nathan before you went out with him? If you had just called me, sis, I would have told you the rumors I've heard lately of his going off the deep end with drinking and drugs."

I finally talked with Brett privately once the busyness of Christmas had passed. I had felt the need for his brotherly council, especially since Brett knew Nathan in high school.

"I'd thought about calling you, but Mom mentioned you were super busy applying to vet school and all. Plus, Nathan was being so incredibly polite and sweet during the weeks leading up to the concert. I remember everybody liking him in high school. He seemed like the perfect date."

Brett paced the room. "Did he try anything? Take advantage of you?"

"No, he gave me a Sprite in the limo, but I think he slipped something in it because I passed out after drinking some of it. I think I was only out for a little while because, by the time we got to the event center, I was awake but groggy. Other couples were in the limo, so we were never alone." I sat on the hearth, feeling the warmth of the crackling fire. "The sweet Christian girl who followed me into the ladies' room got me back to my dorm that night. Her boyfriend drove us."

"How do you know that this girl is a Christian?"

"When I thanked her for helping me, she gave all the credit to God. Nicole and I met up with her and her boyfriend at church the next day. Her name is Leah and her boyfriend's name is Mark. We had brunch with a lot of their friends after church." I pulled up my fuzzy socks then hugged my knees. "What was so extraordinary was that Leah told me that she had once dated Nathan and had a bad experience with him as well. Apparently, he had slipped something into her drink too, and she passed out overnight. He never called her after that."

"Oh, man. Nathan should be arrested!" Brett rubbed the back of his neck.

"Well, he may have been the night of the concert. During the drive from the concert to my dorm, Mark told us that he saw Nathan being cuffed and escorted out of the concert hall. I haven't heard from Nathan since."

"Wow, he sounds deranged. He wasn't like that in high school." Brett shoved his fists into his pockets and looked down, obviously upset. After a long pause, he raised his head, a glimmer shined in his eyes. "So, you've connected with Christian friends at school?"

"Yeah, they've been so supportive, Brett! I'm going to join their Bible study group when we return from Christmas break."

"That makes me feel better, sis. I hate that I can't be there for you, especially for your freshman year."

"You've always been there for me, bro. Like you keep reminding me, you're only a phone call away."

26

"What took you so long to answer your phone?"

"I was helping my dad take down the Christmas tree." I could hear Nicole's dad talking in the background.

"Oh, sorry. You wanna call me back?"

"It's fine. I'm just packing up the ornaments now. We're pretty much finished. What's up?"

"I just heard there's a party tonight on Lake Conroe. Brett, being my protective brother, wants to take us. Wanna go?"

"Sure. What time?"

"Around seven." I stood in my closet, considering my wardrobe options. "What do you think you'll wear?"

"I don't know, something warm. It'll be freezing on the lake."

"I'm so nervous! I hope we don't run into the mean girls."

"Sarah, I can't believe you're still calling them that. You need to get over that whole high school drama. You've got new college friends now."

"I know. Sorry. But I'm having a hard time shaking it off."

"For starters, stop saying sorry all the time."

"Right. See ya at seven."

The party was in full swing by the time we arrived. The moment we opened our car doors, I heard music blaring. There must have been at least a hundred people yelling across the lawns and singing to the music. Out on the dock, a couple of muscular guys threw a thin guy into the lake. That's when I saw the mean girls. They were sitting on a nearby bench, pointing at the splash left by the boy who was underwater. Their cruel laughter brought back haunting memories.

I was relieved to see the thin guy emerge from the water; however, without his cap or glasses.

I eyed Nicole, whose facial features were twisted into an expression of disgust as she scrutinized the dock scene. I took a deep breath and the smell of burning firewood filled my nostrils. I scooted closer to the stone fire pit to seek warmth from the chill of the evening.

As I watched some guys tossing a football, excited chatter swirled around me. I shivered when I felt someone's hand on my neck, massaging it way too forcefully. I turned on my heels. Nathan towered over me, smirking. His green eyes I once found so alluring were now eerily piercing.

"Hey, beautiful. You look incredible tonight. What happened to you at the concert in Austin? We somehow got separated."

Separated? Really? You were hauled off to jail. I was repulsed by his deceit. Before I could formulate my thoughts into words, Brett stepped in front of me.

"Stay away from my sister, Nathan."

Nathan raised an eyebrow, in an expression of arrogance. "Brett! What's up with you, man?"

"You heard me." Brett stood square, planting his feet in the ground. My brother wasn't budging.

I put my hand on Brett's arm. "It's okay. It's not worth it."

Nathan howled, drawing the attention of people scattered across the lawn. "Are you saying I'm not worth it? Ha! You should be thankful I even took you to that concert."

I looked around and saw people staring at me. I saw the mean girls creeping closer. Their stealthy movements resembled those of the wild predatory animals I'd seen on Discovery Channel.

I moved to face my brother. His nostrils flared and his hands clenched into tight fists. "Brett, let's go." My voice was barely audible.

Nicole slipped beside me. Together we blocked Brett from Nathan. I was certain my brother was weighing his options as he shifted his eyes between both of us. It seemed like almost a minute passed before he finally nodded.

I silently thanked God that Brett agreed. As the three of us quietly walked to the car, I heard Nathan's hideous laugh blending with the mean girls' cackles. The harsh sounds echoed after me until I heaved the car door shut.

27

I jolted awake. I took in my surroundings. My bedroom. My heart pounded as I recalled the horrible dream that, moments earlier, had felt so real. Nathan and the mean girls were dunking my face in the lake, laughing their heads off. As weird dreams go, the lake became a toilet bowl, and Leah rushed to my side to save me. I shook my head, chasing away the images. I seriously had to get over my obsession with Nathan and the mean girls . . . and my wounded pride. Yet the memory of last night crept back in. I pushed my palm onto my forehead. *Last night was real.*

My recollections were interrupted by the sweet fragrance of homemade biscuits and maple sausage reaching my nostrils. I flung back the covers and followed the scent down to the kitchen, where Mom was grabbing potholders and hurling the oven door ajar. Brett sat at the breakfast table, huddled over his phone, texting.

Mom beamed a smile across the sun-drenched breakfast room. "Good morning, sleeping beauty." She placed the sheet of biscuits on a trivet then twirled around to stir the eggs on the stovetop. "You two got in early last night. When I heard the door alarm beep, I looked out the window and saw Brett's car parked in the driveway." I grabbed paper napkins and forks from the counter and began setting the table.

Brett looked up from his phone. "Yeah, it's a good thing we left the party early. I just received texts from a couple of friends that Nathan Everett was arrested last night for drug possession."

Brett and I locked eyes. I stood motionless, gripping the forks.

Mom stopped stirring. "Oh no! Poor Lisa! It hasn't even been a year since she lost Nathan's father."

I shot her a look. "What did you say, Mom?"

"Yes, last January, Mr. Everett was killed in a horrible car accident. He crossed the median on I-forty-five and hit an eighteen-wheeler head-on. There was a rumor that he was intoxicated, but we shouldn't trust speculation. It was never confirmed as far as I know." She paused to wash her hands at the sink, the sound of the gushing water filling the silence. Drying her hands, she said, "It's important to always give grace to others, especially those who can't speak for themselves. That whole ordeal was such a shock to our community."

Whoa! I didn't know that about Nathan's dad. A deep and unexpected sorrow washed over me. I never expected my feelings of resentment toward Nathan could turn so quickly.

Mom's frown and furrowed brows showed her worry and concern for the Everetts. She spoke softly. "Lisa must be beside herself. Bless her heart. She must feel like she's losing her son. Lisa and I served together on the high school's Project Graduation parent committee. I'm sure you two remember that alcohol-free celebration after both of your high school graduations. The first year that Lisa and I served together, I got to know Nathan. He seemed like such a good student."

Brett nodded. "Yes ma'am." Brett tucked his phone in his back pocket. "I always thought Nathan was a good guy in high school. I don't think he was ever into drugs or alcohol then. But there've been rumors about him lately."

"Rumors! Hmph! I've never met a gossiper who tried to reach out to the person targeted by the gossip. I should give Lisa a call later. I haven't talked with her since her husband's funeral. I can't imagine the loss she must be feeling."

I helped Mom put the platters of sausage, eggs, and biscuits on the table. Dad entered through the back door, opening the newspaper. He handed Brett the sports section. When we were all seated, Dad said a prayer of thanksgiving.

Mom added to the prayer. "And, Lord, please provide Lisa Everett with Your comfort and peace."

After closing the prayer, Dad gave Mom an inquisitive gesture with palms up and a shrug, and she filled him in on the news of Nathan's arrest. When we finished breakfast, Dad announced he needed to put some tools away in the garage. Brett and I started cleaning the kitchen while Mom went to the study to call Mrs. Everett.

We couldn't help overhear Mom's intonation and inflection through the walls, not her actual words, just the muffled sounds of sorrow.

Brett handed me a scrub sponge as he loaded the dishes into the dishwasher. "I'm glad you stopped me from punching Nathan's lights out last night. I feel bad for him. He must have been high, and probably that's why he was being so offensive toward you. I was in protective brother mode."

"Thanks for being there for me. I don't know what would've happened if you hadn't been. I'm thinking we both wanted to hurt Nathan in a way he'd never forget. I must admit, I've been holding on to resentment against him." I wiped grease from the stove with the sponge. "Now that I know how messed up things are for him and his family, forgiveness seems possible. Remember my mentioning the Christian girl, Leah?"

"Uh, the girl who helped you at the concert?"

"Yes. She called the other night asking how she could pray for me. I told her that I needed prayer for God to help me forgive Nathan. Well, God opened my eyes today to what's going on with Nathan and how his situation has affected, not just me, but a lot of people."

Dad returned from the garage at the same time Mom walked in from the study. Her worry lines had reappeared. Dad adjusted his glasses as he studied her face.

Mom asked, "Do you kids know Nathan's younger sister, Avery?"

Brett narrowed his eyes then shook his head. "No Ma'am. I don't."

"I do." I said. "We had some classes together. She seemed nice and kind of quiet. Is she okay, Mom?"

"Well, she is now. But Lisa said that Avery rode to the party with Nathan, and his car keys were in his pocket when he was taken to the jail. Avery's phone was locked in his car. The police directed everyone at the party to leave after they arrested Nathan. With all the confusion, Avery couldn't find anyone she knew to take her back home. She had to walk on a dark backroad for several miles to reach a gas station so she could call her mother."

Mom paused. Dad put his arm around her. "About the time Mrs. Everett arrived at the gas station, she got a call from Nathan . . . from jail. She and Avery went down to the county jail in the middle of the night. When they arrived, they weren't allowed to see Nathan. They spent the night in the car, parked in the county jail parking lot. Nathan was released on bail this morning."

Mom took a labored breath and sat on the edge of the kitchen bar stool. "I mean, I can't even imagine what that poor woman must be going through."

I stood in place, staring down at the filthy sponge in my hand. I blinked and gathered my thoughts. "How can I help?"

"That's what I asked Mrs. Everett. She simply asked me to pray for all of them." Mom turned to Dad. "Ken, will you lead us in prayer?"

Dad prayed for the Everetts' well-being. By the time we'd said a unified "Amen," I knew I needed to make a phone call. I grabbed my phone and headed to my room.

"Hi, Sarah!"

"Hey, Leah. I hope I'm not catching you at a bad time."

"No, this is a great time. You remember us telling you about the leaders of our community group, the Pates? I'm babysitting their two children, and they're occupied with their crayons. It's so cute to see how older sis is showing younger brother how to hold the crayon."

"Oh, how adorable! How old are they?"

"Becca is four and Zeke is two."

"They're little! Are you sure you have time to talk?"

"Absolutely. They're focused on their drawings right now. I planned to call you later to tell you about my news. I'm engaged! Mark proposed Saturday night."

"What? Oh, Leah, congratulations! Have you set a date?"

"We're thinking sometime in May."

"I'm so thrilled for you and Mark!"

"Thank you. We're thrilled too! I'll show you videos of the proposal when I see you. Mark planned it out so beautifully! How are you? Everything okay there?"

I reclined on my bed. "Well, after your amazing news, I'm sorry to share some sad news. It's about Nathan, and I just hope we can pray about the situation."

"Of course, Sarah. What's going on?"

"I saw him at a party last night. He was coming on to me until my big brother intervened. You remember my telling you about my older brother, Brett?"

"Yeah."

"He took Nicole and me home early because Nathan was being so obnoxious. This morning, we found out that after we left, Nathan was arrested for drug possession. To make matters even worse, I found out that Nathan's dad was killed in a car accident last year." I heaved a sigh. "I feel so bad for his mom and little sister."

"Oh, no! That's awful! His poor mom!"

"You know, Leah, after finding out about his dad's death, which is probably behind Nathan's drinking and drug use, it's getting easier for me to forgive Nathan. I realize God is working on my heart, especially knowing that you prayed that I would find forgiveness."

"Wow, I feel real sorrow for Nathan. I didn't see that coming."

"I know, right? I didn't think I could ever forgive him."

"Yeah, not only forgive him but go beyond that—care about what happens to him and his family."

"Exactly."

"To forgive completely, as Jesus forgives. It's a journey that none of us could do without Christ. So, Sarah, despite what I'm about to tell you, I hope you'll still be on that journey with me. I was going to wait until I saw you, but I think you and I know each other well enough now that I need to go ahead and share. But can you hold on a minute? I should turn the baby monitor on so that I can keep an eye on the children while I step into the next room. I don't want them to hear what I'm about to say."

"Sure." There was a pause on Leah's end. *What could be so bad that the kids shouldn't hear?* I sat up. I crossed my legs. I twirled my earrings. I waited.

Leah came back on. "Okay, they're busy coloring. So . . . the night that Nathan spiked my drink and I passed out in his room, apparently, we had sexual relations. I don't remember any of it."

She paused and the silence was deafening. "Well, now I'm pregnant. The baby can only be his."

"Oh, Leah!"

"I know. It's huge. Actually, I'm beginning to feel huge but that's a good thing because the baby is healthy and loved." After a long pause, she added, "I'm so thankful to God that Mark came into my life right after that time and he's supporting me through this. I thank God for my community group members who've been so supportive."

"Definitely! Hey, sweet friend, thank you for sharing this. For being so transparent."

"You would have eventually found out anyway. You'll see I wasn't exaggerating when I said I'm starting to feel huge. I'm in my second trimester and beginning to have more than just a baby bump."

"Is the pregnancy going well? Are you feeling all right?"

"Oh, yes. The baby is doing well and I'm feeling great."

"When is the baby due?"

"June. Poor Mark will have a very pregnant bride."

"I'm so happy you and Mark are getting married, Leah. You are such a great couple! I'm glad you have such an amazing support network through the community group. I can't wait to be a part of it."

"Me too! Everyone will love getting to know you and Nicole. So, Sarah, how can we pray for Nathan specifically? Is he in jail?"

"He was. Mrs. Everett bailed him out. My mom spoke with her and asked how we might help. Mrs. Everett asked that we keep Nathan and her daughter, Avery, in prayer."

"Then that's what we'll do. Is this a good time that we can pray?"

"Yes, the perfect time."

Leah led us in heart-felt prayer, thanking God for our journey of forgiveness and requesting His provision for the Everett family, for their good and His glory.

I added, "And, Lord, thank You for Leah. She cares for me so well. Please keep her and her sweet baby healthy, and bless her engagement to Mark."

"Amen," we said in unison. I picked up on a slight quiver in Leah's voice.

"Hey, are you all right?"

She laughed. "I'm just crying tears of joy. Plus, my hormones are crazy these days. I'm looking forward to seeing you soon."

"Aw, you too, Leah. Take care of you and that little bundle of joy!"

"Take care, friend. Bye."

28

July 2005
Conroe, Texas

"What are you lookin' at?" she hissed in a low whisper.

Having just barreled around the corner from the sinus relief medicine aisle—I froze—standing face to face with Mallory, the leader of the mean girls. She planted her fist on her hip, which was exposed by her hip-hugging shorts and crop top. Neither Brett nor Nicole was here to save me this time.

"Sorry." *Stop saying sorry!* I cleared my throat and raised my voice. "Actually, I'm not sorry. I was just making my way to the shampoo aisle."

"Whatever!" She turned so abruptly, the object in her grip flew from her hand, spiraling downward.

I stared at the home pregnancy kit that had landed on the polished CVS floor.

She dove to retrieve it then, still crouching, glared back at me. The loathing in her eyes intensified as she twisted her mouth. Was she going to spit on me?

"Mallory! What is taking you so long?" Mallory jumped up at the shrill voice. At the end of the aisle stood a middle-aged woman sporting cat eye sunglasses and leopard print yoga pants. "And what are you doing on this aisle? I thought you had me drive you all the way out here for nail polish! Your dawdling is going to make me late for my yoga class!" She sucked her tongue, making a clicking sound and shaking her head in annoyance. "Your father taking your car away has been more of a punishment for me than for you."

Mallory straightened and faced the woman. With smooth execution, she slipped the pregnancy test into her cross-body purse draped behind her. "I . . .I was just saying goodbye to my friend."

All at once, I had morphed into her friend and a witness to shoplifting.

"Look, young lady, you get your . . . self to the car in one minute or you can walk home."

The woman disappeared and Mallory's head bobbed down. She stared at her feet. The silence between us was broken by the buzz of the CVS door and the clerk's rote, "Have a nice day, ma'am."

I had one minute before Mallory was left behind. I knew I had to say it. "Hey, if you need anything, let me know."

"Oh, like money to pay for this? She poked her purse with her index finger, probably assuming I knew the contents. Her whole being seemed to seethe. "No thanks, I'm fine."

"I meant . . . like . . . someone to talk to. To help in any way."

She studied me, as if I were a difficult math equation. "Why?" Her voice was monotone. It didn't seem like a question. "Why would you be so nice to me, after all . . . I've caused?"

"People have helped me along the way. Thought I'd offer the same."

She still had a bewildered look on her face as she walked away. Her shoulders slumped and her head bent.

I slowly released the breath I'd been holding. I grabbed a bottle of shampoo, the last item on my back-to-college checklist. I made my way to the front counter and went through the motions of checking out.

Handing me my bag of items, the clerk said, "Eleven dollars and twenty cents is your change." He began rummaging through the cash drawer.

"It's okay. Keep the change."

"Pardon?" The clerk looked confused.

"And have a nice day." I wasn't sure if Mallory had paid for the pregnancy test. In case she hadn't, I hoped leaving the money would ease my mind. I knew praying for her certainly would.

On my way home, my thoughts were flying faster than I was driving. Cars zoomed past me and I realized I needed to apply more force to the accelerator.

It had been good being home for the summer, but I was looking forward to getting back to school in August. Never thought I'd leave the comforts of home with such great anticipation.

My first year of college was unbelievable! I'd witnessed God's hand over it all. Some days, I felt like I grew up overnight. But most days, I realized I was still growing . . . with lots of growing pains.

In January, Nicole and I had started meeting with the community group. What wonderful Christian brothers and sisters we'd gotten to know. They accepted me, flaws and all. We completed the study of Luke, an amazing account of how Jesus's life, suffering, death and resurrection fulfilled God's redemptive plan.

One of the most astounding realizations I made came about when we studied Luke 16:15. In that verse, Jesus told the Pharisees, "You are those who justify yourselves before men, but God knows your hearts. For what is exalted among men is an abomination in the sight of God." I finally realized that by caring so much about how I appeared on the outside, I had ignored my inside, which was rotting. I was obsessed with what people thought of me in my futile attempts to put myself and my glory above God and His glory. I learned that God knows my heart and that is all that should matter. Having my heart right with the Lord has eternal implications.

In the spring, Nathan pleaded guilty at his arraignment, with his plea bargain resulting in a sentence of three hundred hours of community service. I think the judge, a family man who knew of Nathan's family situation, was lenient on him.

I don't think it was a coincidence that the judge ordered part of Nathan's community service hours be earned by speaking with the district's students about the dangers of drug and alcohol abuse. Nathan was still serving the remaining required hours through a pregnancy resource center. His responsibilities included hauling and stocking baby furniture. Avery told me that Nathan hoped to earn his marketing degree by completing his last semester close to home, at a Houston university.

Mom invited Mrs. Everett and Avery to a women's Bible study at our church. I joined them in the study when I came home from Austin at the end of May. I enjoyed getting to know Avery. When she studied the Bible, her face lit up. I gave her the Bible that Leah had given me. It had been Brooke's originally. That Bible was making the rounds.

After Bible study one day, Avery shared with me that she was angry with her deceased father. She confided that there was clear evidence of alcohol involvement in his fatal car crash. I hoped Avery could one day go to Austin to visit Leah. I knew Leah would be better equipped than I to mentor Avery about feelings of fatherly abandonment.

Mrs. Everett and Avery attended Sunday services at our church. Nathan came a couple of times during the summer. He mostly kept to himself, but even from a distance, I could see him leaning in during the sermon.

Nathan also contacted Leah to apologize for his "callous behavior" and offered to support the baby in any way that Leah and Mark would allow. Leah said that she had forgiven him and, in time, would allow him to be a supervised part of the baby's life if he could maintain a clean police record.

Mark and Leah were married in May on Town Lake, at the very spot Leah had told Mark of her pregnancy and he vowed to remain by her side.

Leah's father flew in from California to walk her down the aisle. For Leah, that walk symbolized the end of her journey to forgive her father.

It was truly a fabulous celebration of new beginnings and promises, a covenant of love between a husband, a wife, and God.

The baby was born June tenth, a girl, seven pounds eight ounces. Mark and Leah thoughtfully chose her name: Elizabeth Grace Taylor. Elizabeth was Leah's grandmother's name, meaning "God is my oath." Leah told me that she and Mark chose Grace because the baby was a gift from God, His unmerited favor toward them.

The best part was that Brooke and I would get to babysit Elizabeth Grace in the fall, when Leah and Mark went out on date nights or when they just needed time to catch up on their studies.

I prayed that one day Elizabeth Grace would fully embrace the first chapters of her story, that she was adored by God before anyone knew she existed. Those beginning chapters were a testimony of God's protection and provision.

Those first chapters were also about a young mother's obedience to God's will, despite her initial fear and shame. They were about a young man searching scripture to figure out how to be a godly husband to the woman he loved and a devoted father to the adopted child he chose.

Included in Elizabeth Grace's story was a Christian family made up of parents, grandparents, an aunt and friends who would walk alongside her to help her learn about the love of her heavenly Father.

Above all, her story was an account of forgiveness, made whole through Christ's redemptive work. It was a story of God's grace, gifted through Jesus and regifted by those who sought God with their whole hearts.

I was hopeful that the story of Elizabeth Grace Taylor would continue to be a testimony of God's love throughout her life—the life her Creator planned from the very beginning.

As I pulled into my parents' driveway, one of my favorite verses came to mind:

> *"For I know the plans I have for you, declares the Lord, plans for welfare and not for evil, to give you a future and a hope. Then you will call upon me and come and pray to me, and I will hear you. You will seek me and find me, when you seek me with all your heart." (Jeremiah 29: 11-13)*

EPILOGUE

Brooke
August 2023
Dallas, Texas

Finally, the jury returns with its verdict.

The jury foreman stands. "We, the jury, find the defendant guilty on the charge of manslaughter. We, the jury, find the defendant guilty on the charge of statutory rape."

The judge glimpses at the jury members. "Thank you, members of the jury, for your service. You are dismissed." He bangs his gavel and the sound reverberates around the massive courtroom.

Manslaughter usually carries a sentence of up to twenty years as does statutory rape. I'm sure the judge will give this man the maximum on both charges, which may seem harsh, but he's a repeat offender. John and I will plead a reduced sentence contingent on the offender's participation in Christian prison ministry. After all, this man was created in God's image. We feel strongly that he be allowed the opportunity to hear the gospel message and, hopefully, experience the grace and mercy that can come with it.

Sadly, the fifteen-year-old girl was the victim of date rape and manslaughter by poisoning. Throughout this ordeal, her family has been in an extreme state of emotional distress and grief. I can only imagine.

John and I offer them final words of comfort. They thank us for our council. No other words are spoken. Nothing could bring back their daughter. *Lord, please comfort them.*

John and I make our way to Leah, who is seated several rows back. She flew in yesterday morning from Austin to serve as an expert witness in Forensic Toxicology. Her testimony was objective and thorough, bringing clarity to complicated findings regarding the poisonous drug, GHB, which was detected from the victim's forensic analysis.

"Leah, thank you for your excellent testimony." John gives her a side hug.

"Like I told Brooke, it's a mission for me."

"I know the trial ran late, so I won't keep you girls from your lunch date. You're meeting Sarah?"

I nod. "Yeah, at that new café across the street. She just texted that she's there. Hey, let Abbey know that I'll be at y'all's house in the morning to help her refinish the kids' toybox."

"Will do. Thank you again, Leah."

"It was my pleasure." Leah drapes her overnight bag over her shoulder.

As we walk out of the courtroom, Leah grins. "I'm ready for some girlfriend time." I notice Leah's familiar long strides. But her posture is no longer stilted as it had been when we first met. She now has a poised confidence about her.

She and Mark have worked hard to achieve their professional goals, yet they've continued to prioritize family and church commitments. They are parents to Elizabeth Grace, now eighteen years-old; Paul, fourteen; and Shannon, twelve.

We step into the elevator and I push the lobby button. "When Mark picks you up at the café, will he have Elizabeth with him?"

"Oh, yes. That girl still wants me to help her put the final touches on her dorm room, so the three of us will be going back to TCU together. Brooke, one would think she's your daughter the way she has a passion for planning and decorating. It figures since you have been a major influence in her life. You and Sarah helped raise her during those early years." The elevator doors open, and we step out. "Mark and I often talk about how we couldn't have managed without you two babysitting."

"In the little that we helped, the pleasure was definitely ours. You know, Leah, it just dawned on me that I haven't seen Elizabeth in three years, since she served as an attendant in my wedding."

Leah places her index finger on her chin. "Oh, that's right! Elizabeth was at camp when you and Greg came to visit us last year. And I haven't seen Sarah since your wedding. Time flies!"

Since Sarah and I live thirty minutes apart in the Dallas-Fort Worth metroplex, we meet for lunch at least once a month.

Leah and I stop at the crosswalk and wait for the light. The heat rebounds off the pavement, compounding the stifling effect. I retrieve a notepad from my briefcase and fan my face. "Now that Elizabeth will be going to school in Ft. Worth, you can let Sarah and me know when you're in town. We can get together more often."

"Absolutely! Let's plan on that." We cross the street toward the café.

Sarah and her husband, Kevin, met at UT. They settled in Ft. Worth, where Sarah is the financial accountant in Kevin's dental practice. She works mostly from home so she can be with their toddler twins.

Entering the café, I hear screeching across floor tiles as Sarah pushes her chair back. She bolts to Leah and they embrace, rocking side to side.

We sit and talk nonstop, catching up.

The waitress approaches the table with pen and pad. "I'm sorry to interrupt."

"No need to apologize." Sarah's face lights up with a smile. "We're ready to order."

The waitress takes our orders then bustles off.

Sarah scoots closer to Leah. "I was so excited when Brooke told me you'd be in Dallas for this criminal case. How many years have you been serving as an expert witness?"

"Five years." The waitress brings our teas and Leah takes a sip. "For many years, I carried the guilt of not reaching out to other women who had found themselves in situations like mine. The possibility that Nathan could have killed a woman by spiking drinks haunted me for a long time. Thankfully, Nathan has remained clear of any additional crime according to public records. Mark and I have allowed him visitations with Elizabeth Grace, supervised of course."

Leah pauses when the waitress returns to serve our salads. When the waitress leaves, we join hands and I lead us in a prayer of thanksgiving. I feel Sarah and Leah squeeze my hands.

Leah looks up, teary eyed. "Why do I still get emotional around you two?"

Our laughter fills the tiny café.

"You both know I value the sanctity of human life." Leah shifts in her chair. "But years ago, it hit me that I hadn't been active in advocating for the unborn. Brooke, had you not intervened on my nearly aborting Elizabeth and helping me every step of the way, life would have been . . . well, very different." Leah's eyes glisten.

She pauses to take a sip. "Sarah, the time your guy friend asked you to encourage his pregnant girlfriend to carry their baby to term rather than abort, you walked alongside that expectant mother and the baby was born healthy. And I don't know if you've heard that Kara was let go from her OB-Gyn position at a large Chicago hospital when she refused to participate in abortions."

Sarah slowly shakes her head. "No!"

I glance between them. "Well, thankfully, today Dr. Kara Lott runs a flourishing private practice, as we all knew she would." Leah and I share a grin. "But seriously, Leah, you have raised Elizabeth in a way that is certainly pleasing to God. And God, in His perfect timing, has prepared you to be on mission for Christ in your church and community. Also, serving as an expert witness in cases of rape and murder has made a difference in so many lives. You nailed it yesterday for our case, which we've been working on for months."

Sarah covers Leah's hand with her own. "I'm not sure what would have happened to me that night at the concert if you hadn't helped me. You stood by me and changed my life in far-reaching ways. Leah, don't forget how you helped Avery make closure about her feelings of fatherly abandonment. God used your story for the good of me and Avery."

"You both are such incredible friends." Leah dabs her lips with her napkin. "Rest assured that I've come full circle in experiencing God's providence in the preparation, timing, and depth of my servanthood. I'm humbled and feel privileged that He would include me in His plan."

We share the latest news about our husbands, parents, and careers until we're interrupted by the ringing of the bell above the café door. I turn to see Mark holding the door open for Elizabeth, who rushes to our table.

Sarah jumps up to greet her. "Elizabeth! I'm so glad to see you." Sarah narrowly escapes falling backward as Elizabeth engulfs her in a bear hug.

"You too, Aunt Sarah!"

I throw my arms around Elizabeth then pull back to gawk at her height. "Oh my! You've grown up overnight! I've missed you."

She reaches out and draws me close. "Aw! I've missed you too, Aunt Brooke." She looks past me to regard her parents, with a twinkle in her eye. Mark and Leah are kissing hello.

I grasp both of Elizabeth's hands. "When do your classes begin at TCU?"

"Next week. I can't wait! How did the trial go?"

"Your mom was an excellent expert witness. You and your dad must be extremely proud of her."

I look up at Mark when he gives me a side hug. "Hey, Mark! Thank you for letting us borrow your amazing wife for a day. Leah said you and Elizabeth drove up this morning."

"Yeah, I can't believe the Taylor household survived without Leah for twenty-four hours. Nothing caught on fire or exploded." Mark chuckles. "Lizabeth and I left Austin at the crack of dawn. We've already been to her dorm in Ft. Worth to unload the heavy stuff."

"We still need to go to The Container Store to get stackable storage bins before we head back to Ft. Worth," Elizabeth says as she loops her arm through Leah's.

Sarah angles her head to admire Elizabeth and Leah. "You Taylors are the sweetest family!" Mark wraps his arm around Sarah's shoulder. Sarah glances between Mark and Leah. "Where are Paul and Shannon? I thought I'd get to see them too."

Leah smiles. "They're staying with my mom back in Austin. She loves her new home that Mark built for her. She always looks forward to having the kids stay with her, and it's so close, they can just walk over."

"Yeah," Elizabeth says. "Plus, Shannon would have been a pain coming here. She'd want to try on all my new clothes before I could hang them in the closet."

"Lizabeth, speak nicely of your little sister. She thinks you hung the moon," Mark gently reprimands.

Elizabeth nods to her father then turns to Sarah. "Aunt Sarah, I want to offer my babysitting services for the twins now that I'll be living in Ft. Worth." Elizabeth scrunches her nose and grins. "Just putting that out there."

"Absolutely! I will seriously take you up on that offer. We'll pay you extra because they are bouncing-off-the-wall kind of toddlers. Never a dull moment with those two!"

"I love the pictures you've posted on Instagram. Those two littles are precious! They have your beautiful auburn hair." Elizabeth glances at our table and grits her teeth. "I hope we didn't interrupt lunch."

"No, we had just finished." I motion to the waitress for the check. "I hear your mom is going to help you put the final touches on your dorm room."

"Yes, she's going to help me pick out the storage bins I have in mind. We're decorating my room in rose gold florals." She scoots close to me to show me pictures on her Pinterest app.

"I thought it was my job to pick out the storage bins." Mark exaggerates a long frown.

"Sorry, Dad. Still, you're the best dad in the world."

"Well, apparently not when it comes to picking out gold storage bins with roses on them."

Elizabeth bites her lip. "So. . .it's rose gold."

Mark squeezes her shoulders, throwing his head back in a guttural laugh.

"Aunt Brooke and Aunt Sarah, please come see my room when it's finished."

I look into Elizabeth's sparkling blue eyes. "Elizabeth, you're going to be sick of your Aunt Sarah and me by the time you graduate from TCU. We promise, though, to call before we show up at your door."

Elizabeth giggles then wraps us in a three-way hug.

I notice Sarah is tearing up, as I am. How did that tiny helpless infant become such a confident and capable young woman?

Well, Leah and Mark are amazing parents. They, along with family and friends, have instilled in Elizabeth the knowledge of her true identity in Christ. She firmly grasps that she's a valued citizen of God's kingdom, a beloved child of our almighty God, and a growing disciple in Christ. That's why Sarah and I must keep close contact with Elizabeth so we can guide and mentor her through the storms that I'm sure she'll have to navigate in the upcoming years.

But most significantly, it was God who protected Elizabeth and lavished her with the Holy Spirit's indwelling through the redemptive power of Jesus Christ. And He remains present with her today.

I reflect on all of this and give glory and honor to our great God.

> *And Jesus came and said to them, "All authority in heaven and on earth has been given to me. Go therefore and make disciple of all nations, baptizing them in the name of the Father and of the Son and of the Holy Spirit, teaching them to observe all that I have commanded you. And behold, I am with you always, to the end of the age." (Matthew 28:18-20)*

A note from the author:

I wrote this story solely to bring glory to God. If you have had an abortion or assisted someone in abortion, or if you have been apathetic about the sanctity of human life, Jesus offers you forgiveness through his completed sacrifice on the cross. If you question the God-given worth of the unborn, those imprisoned, yourself or others, I pray that God provides council for you and, through the workings of the Holy Spirit, you repent and experience His healing redemption, love, and peace.

DISCUSSION QUESTIONS

1. God created us to be in relationship with Him and with each other. Relationships are broken by sin. Consider the three main characters: Brooke, Leah and Sarah. In the initial introductions of these characters, how are their own perceptions of themselves (i.e. their perceived identities in Christ) flawed?

    Brooke

    Leah

    Sarah

2. As you observe each of these character's journeys, in what positive ways do you see they grow in their relationship with Christ?

    Brooke

    Leah

    Sarah

3. Why is it important that we realize our true identities in Christ in order to better mentor and serve others well?

4. God offers us a forgiveness that is perfect and complete through Christ. As Christians, we are likewise called to forgive others. (Colossians 3:13: "bearing with one another and, if one has a complaint against another, forgiving each other; as the Lord has forgiven you, so you also must forgive.") What are some examples from the story of how forgiveness is shown, not only in words, but through action?

5. Regarding the fathers of Brooke, Leah and Sarah, describe their actions and reactions in how they lead, or fail to lead, their families in a godly manner. Consider Ephesians 5:25: "Husbands, love your wives, as Christ loved the church and gave himself up for her." Why is it important for a woman to marry a man who is grounded in God's Word?

6. Provide examples from the story of:

   A. the benefits of godly mentorship

   B. the benefits of being in Christian community

   C. the power of prayer

   D. the power of knowing and applying scripture

   E. the benefits of having God at the center of marriage

7. God's grace is an undeserved gift given to us, to include His gifts of love, creation and the very air we breathe. His gift of salvation is made available to believers through the redemptive power of Jesus Christ. We, as Christians, are called to regift God's grace to others through care and compassion, while expecting no recognition or thanks in return. Consider 1 Peter 4: 8-10: "Above all, keep loving one another earnestly, since love covers a multitude of sins. Show hospitality to one another without grumbling. As each has received a gift, use it to serve one another, as good stewards of God's varied grace." In the story, what are some examples of grace extended by various characters for the benefit of others?

8. Brooke and Leah showed commitments to be involved in the trial that resulted in the conviction of a sex offender. John could have taken on the case without their assistance. Why do you think it was important for these two women to be involved in the case?

9. Have you, or someone you know, encountered struggles like those experienced by various characters in the story? If so, are the struggles resolving or have they been resolved? If not, what resources are available to help you or the person you know confront these challenges? Do you feel comfortable in sharing your answers with others in your group study?

10. As you reflect on God's grace made available to you, to whom in your personal relationships and in society can you regift grace and what would that look like?

    - through forgiveness?
    - through acts of kindness?
    - through generosity?
    - through love and compassion?
    - through prayer?

Printed in the United States
By Bookmasters